HORSE SENSE

HORSE SENSE

THE STORY OF WILL SASSE,
HIS HORSE STAR, AND
THE OUTLAW JESSE JAMES

JAN NEUBERT SCHULTZ

 CAROLRHODA BOOKS, INC. • MINNEAPOLIS

Carolrhoda Books, Inc.
A division of Lerner Publishing Group
241 First Avenue North
Minneapolis, MN 55401 U.S.A.

Website address: www.lernerbooks.com

Library of Congress Cataloging-in-Publication Data

Schultz, Jan Neubert
    Horse sense : the story of Will Sasse, his horse Star, and the outlaw
Jesse James / by Jan Neubert Schultz.
        p. cm.
    Summary: When his beloved mare is stolen by the James gang after an
attempted bank robbery in the nearby town of Northfield, Will joins the
posse looking for the outlaws.
    ISBN: 1–57505–998–3 (lib. bdg. : alk. paper)
    [1. Horses—Fiction. 2. Fathers and sons—Fiction. 3. Robbers and
outlaws—fiction. 4. James, Jesse 1847–1882—Fiction. 5. Minnesota—
Fiction.] I. Title
PZ7.S3885 Ho 2001
[Fic]—dc21   00–009789

Manufactured in the United States of America
1 2 3 4 5 6 - SB - 06 05 04 03 02 01

TO TERI MARTINI
AND ALLISON CUNNINGHAM

TABLE OF CONTENTS

SOMEDAY
June 1876

"Will! You in there?" bellowed Pa.

Screech! screamed the rusted hinges. The heavy oak door banged against its frame and bright sunlight cascaded into the barn's dim interior. Straw dust and hay shreds billowed into the air, creating an instant haze. A fine-boned chestnut mare whinnied, bolting sideways into the boards of her wooden stall, eyes wide and nostrils flared.

Will, on his knees beside the mare's newborn foal, leaned over to protect it from its mother's startled prancing. "I'm back here," he called softly, calming the mare with his voice. "Come quiet—Star's just foaled!"

Star soon settled down, standing still but trembling. Will slowly rose and stroked her lathered neck. "Steady, girl. Everything's all right."

9

Pa glowered at Will but didn't speak. He walked toward them slowly, looked over the stall at the tiny foal who had just rolled over onto its belly. Will dropped back down on his knees and began rubbing it dry with handfuls of straw.

He talked to Pa, his voice still soft, eyes on the foal.

"Handsome little filly, isn't she, Pa? Long legs, strong haunches, and look at those bright, alert eyes." He grinned as the little newborn managed to get her legs under herself and stand. Star nuzzled her foal, no longer afraid. Will glanced up at Pa. "What do you think of her, Pa?"

Pa watched the youngster wobble to its mother and begin nursing.

"Too fancy. Never grow up strong or heavy enough to pull a plow all day long." He stepped to the double-tie stall of Pete and Penny, the two huge draft horses. They were taller at their shoulders than Pa was altogether. The horses stomped impatient hooves on the straw-strewn floorboards. Pa tossed a couple of ears of corn in their grain box, ruffled their forelocks, then reached for the pitchfork standing behind the manger.

"Time you tend to your chores, Will. Cows are waiting to be milked." He walked to the other end of the barn without another glance at the foal.

Will filled Star's manger with fresh sweet clover hay and went to let the cows in. Pa had pitched the bedding into the stanchions and tied the cows as they entered the barn. Grabbing a bucket and a three-legged stool, Will got set to begin milking. When Pa sat beside the next cow in line, Will said, "Filly's real strong, Pa. Standing already, nursing good. Nice size, too. She'll be a horse you can be proud of."

Pa snorted. "Tomorrow I want you to start grubbing stumps out of that piece of land just south of the pond. If we get it cleared in a week, there'll still be time to plant more corn. Good old Pete is strong enough to pull stumps all day. Penny, too. Good rock-solid horseflesh. Fine, hardworking draft horses. Got legs like stumps themselves."

After a moment's pause, Will said, "I figured we might put a split-rail fence around that clearing. Use it for pasture. It's got good canary grass, clear water in the spring. Just the place for raising horse stock."

"Not using that useless mare you've got!" Pa shot back. "You haven't got enough horse sense to even think of raising horses!" The cows shifted restlessly, unnerved by Pa's harsh voice but apparently used to it. For a while, the only sound was the squirting of milk into the pails.

Will got up and emptied the bucket into the large milk cans they would store in the spring house. "When I turned fourteen, you said I could do a man's work, and I've been working every bit as hard as you. Got a right to raise the kind of horses I see fit, I reckon." Will released the cow and it ambled back out to the corral.

"See fit?" Pa laughed harshly. "I let you work out at the Jones's farm last summer expecting you to bring home one of their fine, strong Belgian colts. All you 'saw fit' to come home with was a scrawny mare that can't do a lick of heavy work! Can't even earn her feed!" Pa released his cow and stomped out the barn towards their small wood-frame house. "Finish bedding down the livestock before you come in for supper!" he called over his shoulder, not looking back.

Will stood a moment, biting his lip, watching Pa walk away. Behind him, Star nickered softly and Will glanced into the stall. The little filly stood with all four legs spread outward. She tilted her head to one side, her bright eyes curious.

Slow and quiet, Will eased open the half-door

and stepped inside. He brushed a few stray straws off Star's shoulder, and she nudged her head against his arm. Reaching up, Will rubbed behind Star's ears, then traced the star on her forehead, bright white against her glossy chestnut coat. She was so fine. How could Pa not recognize how valuable she was?

How he'd worked to earn her! Scything hay, pitching it onto hay wagons, lofting it into the barn. Milking cows, slopping pigs, feeding chickens. Mucking out the barn. No end to it! But at the end of every long day, Star had waited for him at the Jones's pasture gate, nickering when she saw him coming after evening chores. Will had brushed her and groomed her, broke her to ride and trained her to drive, till the late summer day he'd finally ridden her home. And Pa thought she was worthless!

PLANTING
Evening, June 1876

Curls of smoke from Pa's pipe wafted across the front porch, gentle on the evening breeze. Tilting back his large wicker chair, Pa stretched out his legs and propped his boots on the porch railing. Wrens sang in the bushy mock orange, chasing each other in and out of the sweet white blossoms.

Sitting on the top step, Will leaned against the porch post and arranged the jingling horse harness on his lap. Dipping a soft rag into a tin of saddle soap, he rubbed the fragrant salve into the supple harness. He sneaked a glance at Pa, who looked relaxed and comfortable, surveying his neat farmyard in the fading daylight.

Gesturing toward the wheat field, freshly green and newly sprouted, Will remarked, "Small grain is off to a good start this spring. God willing, it should be a good year for cash grain crops."

"Mmmm...," Pa responded.

"You know, we've got enough oats left in the granary to seed down the marshland," continued Will. "Then we'd have surplus oats that we could sell at Ames Mill, and we'd also harvest a crop of straw to sell to the livery stable in Northfield. And we'd still have plenty of grain left to feed our own livestock." Will rubbed the long driving reins, softening the smooth leather straps.

"Hmmm...," hummed Pa. He blew more pipe smoke into the quiet evening air, where it gathered into a blue-gray layer around his head.

The screen door squeaked as Ma came out of the house. She settled into her porch rocker, shaking her long apron into place. She positioned an enameled sieve full of snap peas in her lap and deftly began shelling them. She winked down at Will, and he realized she'd heard him softening up Pa—working up to mention horse breeding again.

"Look at that moon rise," she said, gesturing at the great orange disc rising from the eastern horizon. Her voice had a lovely lyrical quality. Will loved to hear her sing around their small frame house and in the yard. "The Indians called it the 'planting moon.'" She glanced over at Pa, then smiled down at Will.

"Mrs. Heywood came by today to buy some new potatoes and peas," Ma said. "She drove a lovely new surrey, pulled by a fine span of gray mares." *Plink, plink, plink,* the young peas clattered into the metal pan. "She said her husband had to go all the way to St. Paul and spend a pretty penny to get decent driving horses."

Pa grunted, shifting in his chair, disturbing his smoke cloud.

Ma talked blithely on. "Mrs. Heywood carried on and on about how expensive good horses are, and how difficult it is to obtain them." *Plink, plink, plink.*

Pa was blowing smoke rather forcefully now. Will kept his head low, rubbing the harness. A smile turned up the edges of his mouth.

"Farmers have to go a far piece to buy work-horses, too!" Ma's lovely voice sang. "Her husband, Mr. Heywood—you know he's the teller at the First National Bank? He told her a good many farmers and settlers are willing to pay good money for young, healthy horse stock." Plink, plink.

Will watched Pa studying the meadow. The pond reflected the stars beginning to twinkle in the evening sky. Maybe Pa wouldn't plow it up. Maybe he'd pasture it yet.

"You suppose, Pa? If we had a pair of bred mares . . ." He saw a frown draw Pa's eyebrows together and hurried to add, "We could raise a pair every year to sell. Couldn't use Pete for breeding, of course, him being a gelding. Penny could drop some nice foals, but she's just grade. Her foals wouldn't be worth as much as purebreds. And if I trained the offspring to pull a wagon or a plow, they'd fetch a right handsome price." Will hoped he hadn't pushed Pa too far. He held up the soft shiny harness, inspecting it carefully but keeping one eye on Pa.

"Mebbe so," conceded Pa. "But there's a great many things to consider here. We've got a fine farm already—selling grain, milk, and eggs, some beef. Changing over to a stock farm involves a lot of expense. Lots more work required while we're switching. It'd take some thinking and planning. It don't do no good to jump right into something and then find yourself in over your head." He stood and tapped his pipe over the porch railing, scattering the ashes in the dirt, then went directly inside, not waiting for any discussion of the matter.

Will and Ma exchanged glances as Pa stomped up the stairs to the bedroom. Soft moonlight shone on Ma's hair, pulled into a bun as neat as it had been that morning.

"Now don't go getting your hopes up, Will," she said. "Just like this here pea seed, when you plant an idea, it takes a while before anything sprouts."

But Will's mind raced with ideas about raising horses. They could make so much more money raising and selling horses than they could by just farming. He imagined the meadow filled with beautiful big draft horses grazing on waving green prairie grasses, his days spent training and grooming them.

And not just workhorses. Why not driving horses? Maybe he could find a way to get Star bred again this summer!

ABOUT TIME!
Mid-August 1876

Harnesses jingling, Pete and Penny stepped backward into the hitching frame of the wagon. Will lifted the wooden wagon tongue and attached it to the steel hames on the horses' collars, then he connected the eveners behind the horses. Next, standing on his tiptoes beside Pete, Will reached across the big gelding's broad back, checking the harness. Pete kept shifting his weight from foot to foot, a rolling motion that made Will have to sway to line up the reins through the metal rings. Penny, next to Pete, was restless too. She was pawing a big hole in the ground, swishing her tail in rhythm with the movement of her hooves.

"Whoa there, Pete. We'll soon be on our way," Will said. The early morning sun still cast a long shadow as he walked around to the right of the team to adjust Penny's harness. "Took almost two months for Pa to finally decide to go to a horse auction," he muttered to her. "About time!"

Penny shook her big head, rattling her collar seemingly in agreement with Will. He patted her shoulder and brushed her white mane off her copper-colored neck. Hearing the squeaky screen door, he looked up to see Ma bustle down the steps to the wagon.

"Lunch," she said, smiling. She held out a large wicker basket covered with a red-and-white ging-ham cloth.

Will tucked the basket under the wagon seat. It smelled like fresh baking-powder biscuits. He grinned at Ma, the dimple in his cheek just like hers.

Tilting her head, hands on hips, Ma inspected him. She dusted imaginary specks off his white homespun shirt and straightened his suspenders. She reached up to his forehead, but Will stepped back and jammed his felt hat over his dark blond hair.

"What's taking Pa so long?" Will asked. "We should have left at sunup."

Ma repositioned his cap, tucking in loose ends. "Don't be so impatient, Will," she said. "You know your Pa likes to take his time, to have everything thought out and planned. Just relax and enjoy the day."

Pa stepped out the door. Dressed in a white shirt buttoned up to the neck, his black Sunday coat, and his cleanest pair of work pants, he reached down to give a final rub to his already-polished boots. He climbed into the buckboard as Will jumped up to the wagon seat. Pa slapped the reins across the horses' backs and they set off for Mankato at a brisk trot.

"Take care now," Ma called after them, waving.

Still damp with morning dew, the countryside sparkled in the early sunshine. Well-tended farmhouses, tucked between lakes and marshes, had wood smoke rising from their stone chimneys. Fields of corn and grain, pastures, and meadows were quilted between uncut wooded areas. Wild roses bloomed alongside the road, scenting the breeze. The passing wagon set a flock of crows to cawing and scolding.

"Good growing season," commented Pa. The corn in the fields was chest high, setting fat ears on strong stalks. "Hot days and nights will fill out those kernels."

"Wheat is ripening, too," said Will. A field of

yellow grain billowed in the slight wind like waves on a lake. "Lots more farms settled around here every year."

Pete and Penny trotted briskly past a farmer urging a balky mule down his driveway. Kicking and whacking didn't seem to help him any. The mule didn't budge even when the farmer pulled on its reins and yelled at the stubborn animal.

"Maybe he's on his way to Mankato to trade his mule for a riding horse," said Will, suppressing a laugh. "It's folks like him who'll buy horses from us once we get a breeding herd."

"Don't you ever stop and think?" asked Pa. "Where d'you expect we'd keep a breeding herd? If we buy a team today, we'll have to build another double-tie stall and move our grain storage to the seed house. It's not as simple as buying more horses. You have to plan how to keep them. It all takes money!"

Will's mouth drew into a tight line.

"Your mare and filly eat their share, too, and I don't see you putting them to any good use," continued Pa, slapping the reins. Penny shook her head but kept her pace steady.

"Pa, Star's my riding horse. I ride her to school," said Will. "If we had a buggy, Star could pull it. We could take Ma to church in fine style."

Will clamped his jaw shut. If he said any more, Pa would turn and go back home.

It was not yet noon when they drove down the winding road into the Minnesota River Valley, to the bustling town of Mankato. Pa headed toward the livery stable on Rock Street. A group of wagons and teams was secured under a shady stand of elm trees.

"Tend to the team, Will," said Pa. He jumped off the wagon and pulled his hat down tightly over his brow. With his unlit pipe held in his teeth, he sauntered off. "I'll check out the auction stock."

Will led Pete and Penny to the watering trough.

"Pa seems to have calmed down some, but it wouldn't surprise me none if Pa decided everything cost too much and we went home with nothing," he told Pete, scratching the horse's ears as it drank. "I sure hope Pa finds a team that pleases him. Good thing we heard about this auction. He never would have gone up to St. Paul." Tethering the team under a large shady elm, Will threw a fly harness over their backs and gave them each a feedbag of oats.

Pete and Penny secured, Will walked down a rope picket where the horses to be auctioned were tied. All kinds of horses. Handsome workhorses, old and tired workhorses. Fancy driving horses, riding horses of all sizes and colors, even ponies. Farther down the lane, Pa was arguing with an owner, haggling prices already.

Wheet! A sharp whistle from the auctioneer silenced all chatter from the milling crowd. Will ran to catch up to Pa and find seats by the auction ring. About time!

Will stayed close behind Pa, who elbowed his way through the jostling crowd. They soon found a space on the long boards that rested on log chunks, providing seating for the auction-goers. The plank seats, surrounding a dirt showring, filled quickly with city and farm folks, all of them talking and laughing and arguing. The ruckus quieted when the auctioneer, a barrel-chested man with a big handlebar mustache, climbed onto a board platform spanning two upturned barrels. He whacked the barrels with a heavy wooden cane and his deep voice boomed out, "Gentlemen! Colonel Cooper at your service. All sales final. Pay my clerk over yonder."

The colonel gestured with his cane at a bespecta-cled young man wearing black armbands and carry-ing a sheaf of papers and a burlap money bag. Next the colonel whipped his big cane around to point out an opening in the showring, where a stable-boy led out a beautiful gray gelding.

"Gentlemen! A fine lady's mount, gentle and dependable, trained to sidesaddle. What am I bid?" His eyes expertly scanned the crowd as he rapidly called amounts and pointed both hands in different directions at raised arms, waving hats, and shouts of bids. The numbers rose quickly, then stalled.

"Sold!" the colonel yelled. "To the distinguished Mr. Johnson."

"Poorest excuse for a horse I ever saw," Pa mut-tered to Will. "Sinful waste of money."

Pa's remark brought a chuckle from behind. Will turned around. He saw two darkly tanned men with leather hats shading eyes that were used to bright sunlight. They wore high riding boots with spurs. Their long linen coats—dusters—were uncommon, usually worn by cattlemen and horse herders. They must have come from quite a dis-tance. The man with darker hair and eyes grinned at Will.

"Folks will pay plenty for the kind of horse they

need," he drawled, his accent very different from what Will was used to hearing.

Will nodded politely, his attention drawn back to the ring. He hoped Pa would notice how highly folks valued fine-blooded horses—like Star. A matched pair of black mares pranced skittishly into the ring, the groom holding their halter ropes tightly.

"Young, green-broke for driving," called the auctioneer. "A splendid opportunity for the experienced driver." Quickly he began reeling numbers. At once, several well-dressed gentlemen called and waved their bids. Talking nonstop, pointing repeatedly, the auctioneer kept the bids increasing. At the briefest pause, he yelled, "Sold!" keeping the crowd eager and excited. Will sat at the edge of his plank, watching the bidding, although bids were signaled too fast to really follow.

A handsome, well-mannered bay was brought out next. The black mane and tail were beautiful against its carefully brushed brown coat. Pa sat back and folded his arms across his chest.

"Enough of these fancy horses," Pa muttered, none too softly. "Bring out the working livestock." Will sat back on his bench. Pa didn't like these horses at all—it didn't matter to him how fine they were or how much money they were worth.

The dark-eyed stranger behind them motioned with his head to the crowd sitting in the front rows. "See all the gents in suits? They're the ones with the money. They want driving horses. The auctioneer is just giving the rich folks what they want," he drawled. "Not smart to make them wait, right, Frank?"

The taller stranger, who looked enough like the other to be his brother, laughed briefly. "Lots of money changing hands today," he remarked. Looking at Will, he asked, "Got good secure banks in this town?"

"I suppose so," answered Will. "But we don't live here. We came down from Northfield."

"That so?" asked Frank. "We've heard of your prosperous little town. Big mill, colleges, rich farmers, good bank . . ."

The colonel's call of "Sold!" brought Will's attention back to the auction. Another riding horse, complete with saddle, pranced out next. With a snort, Pa got up and walked out, not worrying if he stepped on anyone's toes. Will jumped up and hurried after him.

He'd better calm Pa down, or he'd leave for home.

Pa went directly to the wagon in the shade of the elm, its overhanging branches swayed by a cool breeze. Will was just a step behind him. Pa climbed up on the wagon seat, reached around behind him and lifted out Ma's basket. Will climbed up on the other side, taking that Pa was just hungry as a good sign.

When Pa lifted off the cloth, smells of fried chicken and biscuits wafted up, making Will's mouth water. Pa settled back in the wagon seat and propped his boots up on the front boards, a plate of chicken on his lap and a drumstick in his hand. Directly in front of them stood a line of draft horses tied to a rope picket.

Big, beautiful animals. Shiny black Percherons, compact and muscled. A pair of stallions, speckled blue over gray, very pretty. Two white geldings, looking strong and regal. And Belgian mares, coppery gold, with flowing white manes and tails, so handsome that Will couldn't help but admire them. If Pa wouldn't buy pleasure horses for breeding stock, perhaps he'd bid on animals like these. Will knew he couldn't push Pa into a decision or talk too much at him. He got too bucky. He'd need to think it was all his own idea.

"Those Belgians sure are pretty, Pa. Must be

purebred breeding stock," Will said carefully.

Pa studied the big gentle horses. "Probably cost more than any animals here."

"But their colts would bring a top price, too," Will said, reaching into Ma's basket for another piece of chicken. He thought a minute, then continued, "They'd pay for themselves in two, three years. Takes money to make money."

Pa snorted. "Easy for you to say. Did you figure how much stud service would cost? We'd have to use a Belgian stallion to get purebred colts." But he pursed his lips, studying the mares.

"We might get a stud colt," Will countered. "You'd make money in the long run."

"We'll see what they go for," said Pa. "Can't spend money we haven't got."

Will didn't say anything more, and neither did Pa. Will kept glancing sideways at him, angry. Pa never took a chance. Took so long deciding that he'd never bid at all.

BIDDING
Mid-August 1876

Finished with lunch, Pa wandered toward the line of picketed horses, stopping by each and every draft horse to give it a personal inspection. Will wandered on down Rock Street, keeping a watch out for good-looking riding horses. Just ahead, tied to a hitching rail, stood four strong tall horses, saddled and half-dozing in the shade of the trees. Will stopped and stared. They couldn't be for sale, not tied back here and saddled. They must belong to folks come to watch the auction.

Approaching the horses, Will stepped in front of the rail so he could see all four at once. They were far better than anything offered in the auction. A fine bay gelding looked back at him with interest. His reddish brown coat had a glossy sheen and his black mane and tail were combed smooth.

Expensive saddle, too. A stallion, slightly taller than the bay, stood next in line. He also had a brushed black mane and tail, but his coat was buckskin, a tawny beige. Another bay was tied to the rail, and beside it, a grayish brown—dun—gelding. All were handsome, quality horses. Will reached out to stroke the buckskin's neck.

"Hey there, boy," he said to the stallion.

The soft nose nuzzled Will's shoulder, the horse obviously used to being handled. Will ducked under the hitching rail beside the stallion, running his hands down the long curved neck, his eyes glancing over the strong muscles rippling to dislodge flies. "You're the finest horse I've ever seen," he said to the buckskin.

A jangle of several spurs startled Will, and he ducked back under the rail, stepping away from the horses. Four men in long linen coats strode toward him. They scowled at Will, who stepped farther back as he recognized two of the men.

The one called Frank stared at him.

"It's just the kid from the auction," he drawled. "I don't think he's about to steal our horses." He laughed and so did the others.

The men reached for the bridle reins of their horses and mounted up—all except the dark-eyed man who had talked to him at the auction ring. He flipped up the stirrup on the buckskin and began tightening the cinch. He grinned at Will, all friendly-like. "Looks like you prefer fine riding horses, not those slow, overgrown workhorses your pa favors."

The others rode off. "We'll be at the saloon, Jesse," Frank called back, whirling his dun gelding around and away.

"Yes sir," said Will, answering Jesse's remark. "I hope to raise fine horses. I've got a nice chestnut mare back home. Should get her bred soon." Will's eyes appraised the buckskin stallion as Jesse pulled its cinch tighter. His mind raced—he should get her bred to a fine stallion like this one. "Pa would never agree to having her bred, though," continued Will. "Costs too much. All Pa ever thinks about are expenses." He patted the buckskin's smooth, sleek neck.

Jesse dropped the stirrup and gave the stallion a light slap on the shoulder. He pulled a tobacco pouch and papers out of an inside duster pocket and started to roll a cigarette.

"Sounds as if your Pa is a cautious man. Can't see beyond his own eighty acres. Never takes a risk." He struck a match and lit his cigarette.

"That's exactly what he's like!" said Will. "You can't tell him anything."

Jesse blew smoke into the air.

"You'll never get anywhere without taking chances," he said. "A man's got to go after what he wants. Can't worry about other folks." He poked his finger in Will's chest. "And don't worry none about how much a good horse might cost. Get the best you can however you can. A good horse can save your life."

Tossing his cigarette on the ground, he grinned at Will. "You say you live at Northfield? Maybe we'll be up that way."

Will grinned back. "Would you?" He reached out his hand to Jesse. "I'm Will Sasse. My pa's Henry Sasse. We're just southwest of Northfield off the Dundas road. Come on by."

"Might just stop in and check out your mare," said Jesse, shaking Will's hand. Then with a quick, easy leap, Jesse was in the saddle. His linen duster flared open as Jesse whirled his horse. A very large Colt revolver was strapped at his waist.

Will stood in the dusty street staring at Jesse galloping away. The dusters, the horses and saddles, the guns. They were cowboys, probably from Dakota Territory.

"Going! Going! Gone!" A burst of applause followed the call at the sale ring. Startled, Will ran back to the auction. What if that was Pa's sale? He dashed into the circle of plank seats, dodging outstretched legs and log chucks. Sitting alongside Pa, he noticed two fine Percheron mares being led out of the ring, bright sunlight gleaming on their shiny black coats. Pa wore a slight, satisfied smile.

"Pa?" Will asked. "How long have they been selling the workhorses? Did you bid on those?"

Pa slowly turned his head and looked at Will.

"Quite a while," he said, "and no, I didn't." His voice was low and tense. "And where have you been? I thought you came here to see the auction." He said nothing more, turning his back on Will as a fine pair of Belgian mares was led into the ring.

The mares stepped high, holding their heads alertly, watching their surroundings with curiosity. Their golden coats were brushed smooth and silky, their snowy white manes and tails waving like a spring waterfall. The muscular bodies were strong and well proportioned. A collective "Ahh" went up from the crowd.

At the first call for bids, Pa touched the brim of his hat but said nothing. The calls rose quickly. Pa never changed expression, just gave a slight nod when the auctioneer's arm beckoned in his direction. The bids came slower.

Will looked around, trying to see who was bidding. Who had the top bid? Pa? Then Will felt frantic, wondering did the auctioneer recognize Pa's slight nods as bids? The bids slowed. The auctioneer stopped calling for a moment to point out the mares' special features.

"Bred to the owner's fine Belgian stallion, folks. You'll be getting four horses for the price of two!" He paused as the crowd laughed, then continued, "Trained to work and trained to drive. Pretty a team as a man could want. Now, who'll give me two hundred dollars?" The Colonel's call rolled into a continuous rumble of numbers. A flurry of renewed bidding followed, Pa still nodding at times, still expressionless. Finally it slowed again.

"Going? Going?" said the Colonel. Will held his breath. He didn't know who had the last bid.

"Gone! To the gentleman in the near row!" the Colonel yelled, pointing at Pa. Several farmers in the crowd called out their congratulations.

As the mares were led out, Pa rose and walked out too. Will followed.

"Pa! They're beautiful. They're worth every penny." Will talked fast, trotting behind him. Pa went to settle up with the clerk who was keeping accounts on a board stretched out over two nail kegs. Will walked over to see the mares close-up. He petted and fussed over them, ruffling their manes and forelocks, running his hands down their faces, rubbing the soft velvety noses. They nuzzled him back, calm and gentle.

Receipt in hand, Pa came to claim them. A farmer, tall and muscular as the horses, shook his hand. "Glad you got them, Mr. Sasse. I know they're in good hands."

Mr. Jones owned the Belgians? Well, of course. Will had seen horses like these at the Jones's farm when he worked there, but not this nice pair. They must have been yearlings then.

"Bring the mares over the next time you need stud service," Mr. Jones told Pa. "I'll give you a special price." He clapped Pa on the back.

"Hello there, Will," he said. "How'd that little filly work out for you? Did she grow up to be worth all your work?"

Pa snorted and led the Belgians back to the buckboard. Watching him go, Will said, "Star's real fine, Mr. Jones. I've trained her to ride and to drive. Made something out of her, all right. Foaled back in April; a beautiful filly."

"Good for you," said Mr. Jones. "Glad to hear it." He walked back to the ring.

Pa was tying the mare's lead ropes to the back of the wagon when Will got there. Business accomplished, Pa was ready to leave. Will untied Pete and Penny and climbed up to the wagon seat. Pa was refilling his pipe. He had said hardly a word to Will since he had returned to his seat in the auction ring. Will didn't know how to start the conversation again.

Driving the team up the wooded ravine road out of the valley, Will said, calm and quiet, "They're fine breeding stock, Pa. You got the best. Can't wait to see their foals in the spring."

Pa nodded, still not saying anything.

Will sat thinking. Pa must have talked with Mr. Jones while he was with Jesse. Suddenly his mind flew back to his own hopes and to Jesse's buckskin stallion.

Frank and Jesse were sure to come to the farm, probably any day now. Will had to think how he could pay the men a stud fee to get Star bred again. Sure didn't look forward to discussing that with Pa.

VISITORS FROM MISSOURI
September 1, 1876

Black-eyed Susans nodded and waved in the warm, late summer breeze, bumblebees buzzing around their orange and black blossoms. The bees took no notice of Will standing knee-deep in the wild-flowers, chopping and shaping a fence rail with his small hatchet. He straightened up, took off his hat, and wiped his sleeve across his sweating forehead. Hatchet in one hand, hat in the other, he looked back with satisfaction at the row of new fence that enclosed the meadow pasture. Then he turned to look down the road to gauge how much fence still needed to be built.

Hoofbeats? He cocked his head and listened. Several horses, he guessed. No wagons. He stepped out of the patch of flowers onto the roadside.

Coming around the bend past a grove of oak trees, four riders cantered abreast down the center of the road, all wearing white linen dusters and leather hats, riding as easy as if they'd been born in the saddle. The strong handsome horses were barely winded, looking as if they could run steady all day long. Will recognized the horses before he did the riders. He waved his hat at the men.

They reined up and stopped beside him. Jesse leaned on his saddle horn. "Will Sasse, this your spread?" he drawled, grinning.

"Yes sir," answered Will. "Been watching for you." Hatchet still in hand, he pointed down the road to the farmyard. "Come get a drink. Sit a spell." His glance went from Jesse to the buckskin stallion. Such a handsome animal.

"Sure could use some cool water," said Jesse, "and food, too." The four men walked their horses toward the farmstead, Will leading them on foot. Pa came out of the barn to greet the strangers. Dismounting, they shook hands and introduced themselves.

"This here's Frank," said Jesse. "There's Cole and Clell, and I'm Jesse." He looked around the neat farmyard. "Mr. Sasse," he said, "could we buy food for the horses and ourselves?" He reached under his duster and drew out a fat wad of green-backs.

"I reckon so," replied Pa, eyeing the bills. "Water your horses yonder at the trough. I'll let the missus know there'll be company for supper." With a nod, he walked up to the house.

Will pumped fresh water into the horse trough as the men unsaddled their mounts and tossed the saddles onto the corral fence. The horses, their coats somewhat damp with sweat, drank deeply. Will watched the stallion. It looked to be a quarter horse, like Star. They had the same strong neck and chest, muscled in the haunches. The buckskin was bigger than Star, of course. Taller.

"That the mare you spoke of?"

Will turned to see Jesse standing with his arms crossed over the top rail of the corral, looking at the pastured horses. Penny and Pete and the new Belgians, Molly and Mae, grazed placidly, but Star had caught the scent of the visitors' horses. She stood by the creek, head held tall, ears pricked toward them. "That's my mare," Will said, pride in his voice. "Her name's Star." How pretty she looked, standing so alert.

Frank and Clell had headed for the shade of the front porch, but Cole noticed Jesse's interest and came over to watch Star. "Right fancy mare," he commented.

"She's real nice, all right," said Jesse. Star's little filly pranced around its mother, chasing butterflies. Star whinnied but stood still. "Quarter horse, isn't she?"

Will nodded. He could tell that Jesse liked Star, that he could see she was special.

"No finer breed than quarter horses," said Jesse. He glanced at Cole and they grinned at each other. "Tell you what, Will. After you've given our horses a grain ration, why don't you just turn them all out into the pasture? We'll be an hour or two at supper. Might as well let the horses graze." The stallion was now nickering at Star.

Cole chuckled, one foot on the lower fence rail.

Will looked into Jesse's laughing eyes. Jesse was offering to let the stallion run with Star. "Can I? But—I can't pay you anything for stud service." He looked from Jesse to Cole and back again.

Jesse laughed. "Just turn them loose."

"Let nature take its course," added Cole.

Will hesitated. "I should ask Pa if it's all right."

"No reason to," said Jesse. His dark eyes snapped. "Make up your own mind, now. What do you want?"

"I want Star bred," said Will, afraid Jesse would change his mind. "Been wanting it all summer. But—"

"Don't worry none about details," said Cole. "Your Pa can't do anything about it once it's done."

Jesse was watching Star. "Real nice mare, for sure."

"Quality stock," agreed Cole. "Now let's go see what's for supper. We haven't eaten all day." He and Jesse turned and strode toward the farmhouse, leaving Will alone.

Will ran to the granary and grabbed a pail full of oats. Just inside the corral fence was a feedbox he poured the grain into, adding a few ears of corn. Taking the bridles off the horses, he loosed the animals into the pasture. The two bays and the dun went to the grain box, but the stallion galloped straight to Star.

Will climbed up and sat on the top rail, watching Star and the buckskin get acquainted till Pa called him to supper. He'd better not say anything to Pa about what he'd done. Pa'd have a conniption if he knew.

The travelers sat on the porch enjoying a smoke when Will came up. The smell of fried ham drifted out the kitchen window. Two fresh apple pies cooled on the sill. Pa had found a jug of applejack to tide them over until Ma had supper ready. The men seemed to be enjoying the hard liquor, trading horse stories with Pa.

Boiling egg-coffee added to the delicious smells floating out the window when Ma came to the door, wiping her hands on a flour sack dish towel.

"Supper's on the table," she said with a smile.

The men quickly downed their applejack and tossed their hats on their chairs, but they kept their dusters on. Inside they sat on the bow-back chairs and dug into the food.

Will sat next to Frank, and when Frank reached for the bowl of boiled potatoes, Will noticed a bulge around his hips. Frank still wore his gun. Will looked at the others. They all wore guns. Will hoped that Ma wouldn't notice. She didn't allow guns in the house at all—even made Pa keep his rifle in the woodshed. And these were hand-guns, not hunting rifles. He turned to look at Ma. She was busy at the cookstove, boiling another pot of coffee.

Buttering Ma's fresh-baked bread, Pa asked, "What are you fellows doing in these parts? Sounds like you're from the South."

"Yes sir, we're from Missouri," said Frank.

"We're here aiming to buy horses and cattle, maybe land."

"Thinking of settling around here?" asked Pa.

"We might," said Jesse, his drawl slow and soft. Cole and Clell, intent on wolfing down the food, never looked up.

"Tell me about Northfield," continued Jesse. "There looks to be lots of prosperous farms hereabouts. And we've heard about the big flour mill. What about the bank? Safe place to keep our money?"

Pa shrugged, spooning sugar into his coffee cup.

"Reckon it's safe enough. Everyone banks there. Got a new time-lock vault."

Will scarcely ate, watching the men and listening to the talk. Pa didn't like interruptions, so Will said nothing. After finishing Ma's pies, the men went back onto the porch for another smoke and another round of applejack. The sun was getting low.

"Time we get on to Northfield," said Jesse, putting on his hat. "Come on, boys." He pulled out several greenbacks and handed them to Pa. He tipped his hat to Ma, who was standing in the doorway. "Fine supper, Ma'am."

Will went with them to the pasture gate. Jesse whistled, sharp and loud. His buckskin raised its head, whinnied and trotted up to the gate. The others followed. Will watched Star closely. She nickered, then pranced away across the pasture. Will felt sure she had been bred by the buckskin.

The travelers quickly saddled and mounted the horses, then started to ride back to the road. Jesse stopped a moment beside Will, who looked up at him.

"How can I thank you?" Will asked.

Jesse grinned. "Maybe someday you can do something for me. Good luck." He spurred the buckskin and galloped down the road.

Pa came up beside Will, counting the bills in his hand.

"Fine fellows," he said. "Paid cash on the barrelhead."

Looking at the money in Pa's hand, Will felt his elation subside. Should he tell Pa about Star and the stallion? No, he decided. Not yet.

A TRIP INTO NORTHFIELD
Early Afternoon, September 7, 1876

"Whoa, Pete. Easy now, Penny." Will hauled back on the reins to make the team edge the buckboard up alongside the raised loading dock. The clapboard walls of Ames Mill loomed over the wooden platform, its shade providing cool air on this warm afternoon. Pa and Will climbed into the back of the wagon and hoisted grain sacks out onto the dock. They didn't speak. The Cannon River rushing through the mill's waterwheel and the turning grindstones whooshed and clattered and screeched.

"Does Mrs. Sasse need more wheat ground?" boomed a voice used to making itself heard over the mill racket. "You've got a lot of grain there."

Heaving a heavy gunnysack onto the platform, Will saw the miller, brushing his large hands on a white canvas apron. The muscular miller bent over and lifted the grain sacks into a large wheelbarrow.

"Howdy, Bill," replied Pa, stacking another sack on the dock. "We've got enough flour for quite a spell. These are oats. We're wanting to sell the grain outright. I trust you can use them?"

"Reckon so," answered the miller. "Folks are always looking to buy grain." He wheeled the barrow of grain inside the mill.

Will followed him through the large double doors and helped stack the grain sacks on wood planks.

"We're taking the straw bundles to the livery," Will said loudly. "Mr. Davis needs straw. Said that he was boarding quite a few horses." The fine flour dust hanging in the air made Will sneeze. He rubbed his nose, glad to follow the miller into a small office where the flour dust had settled onto a long wooden table.

"Twelve sacks in all, about twenty-five pounds each," shouted Pa. The grindstones were just the other side of the wall.

Bill nodded, brushing flour off his arms and shirt, creating a little dusty cloud. He opened his cash drawer and counted out bills to Pa in payment for the grain. Shaking hands with him over the deal, Pa and Will left.

Will drove the team across an arching metal bridge that spanned the river to the east section of Northfield. The river was flowing fast through the waterwheel, the screech of its gears accompanied by the splashing water. Directly across the bridge was Mill Square. Facing the square on the south side was a handsome stone two-story office building named the Scriver Block. A narrow alley separated it from two hardware stores, Mr. Allen's and Mr. Manning's.

"Pull up to Manning's store, Will," directed Pa.

Entering the store, Will looked at the shelves surrounding the walls, filled with tools of every description, nails, and farm supplies, and wondered what Pa wanted in here.

The tall bearded proprietor, Mr. Manning, stood beside a large glass showcase displaying rifles, handguns, and shotguns. Pa walked up and studied the guns. Pointing to his choice, he said, "Let me see that Winchester."

Will crowded up close. Nodding and smiling, Mr. Manning reached inside and got the gun Pa indicated. "Good choice for hunting," Mr. Manning said. "Good long range."

Pa inspected it closely, turning it over in his

hands. He opened and closed its chamber, sighted down the barrel and then handed it to Will.

"Think you can get some wild game for the larder with this?" Pa asked. Will reached slowly for the gun, feeling the fine burl wood of the stock, the burnished steel of the barrel. It was well made and well balanced. He looked up at Pa.

"This could drop a deer way the other side of the meadow," he said, his voice a little husky. Peeling off a couple of bills, Pa instructed Mr. Manning, "Hold it for us. We'll pick it up after we finish the rest of our business." He chuckled. "Wouldn't do to take it into the bank."

Will handed the gun back to Mr. Manning, never taking his eyes off it. Following Pa out to the wagon, Will scarcely noticed where he walked. His mind was on deer trails in their woods. He thought of a large spreading oak tree that was easy to climb, had good view of the ravine, and plenty of covering branches. It would make a good spot for a deer stand.

Pa drove the wagon up Mill Square and turned north on Division Street, heading toward the livery stable. "Seeing as how we had some extra money," Pa said, "I thought we should get you a good rifle. If we get enough game to fill the smokehouse, we might not have to butcher the bull calf this winter."

Will sat up straight and looked at Pa. "Fine idea. I'll fill that smokehouse! Thank you, Pa. It's a wonderful rifle. I'll treat it proper. It's a respectable gun."

Penny and Pete broke into a trot as they neared the livery. A pungent, horsey smell of animals and hay and manure drifted out of the stable. Several horses were tied in stalls while several more milled about in the corral. A few buggies and wagons were lined up along the outside of the barn. Pa reined up in front of the hitching rail, got off the wagon, and tied the team.

"Mr. Davis," said Pa to the stable owner, who had come out of the livery, "we brought you some fresh straw."

The slim liveryman leaned his pitchfork against the outside wall and looked into the wagon barn. Golden bundles of straw tied with twine were piled behind the wagon seat. "Good," he said. "Glad to have it."

Will jumped down and grabbed a bundle under each arm, the prickly stalks poking through his shirt. He carried them inside, stacking them where Mr. Davis indicated, not too close to the stalls. Several horses whinnied, smelling the fresh oat straw. Will asked Mr. Davis, "Have you met the travelers from down South?"

"The cattle buyers from Missouri?" said Mr. Davis. "They've bought grain here a couple of times. They sure have fine horses, exceptionally well trained. Probably fast as all get out." He brushed straw off his pants and shirt. "They sure know good horseflesh. Can't understand why they haven't bought any livestock from anyone hereabouts."

Will suspected this was because no one had the quality stock they wanted. That would all change when he got his own breeding herd! He brushed straw off himself, too.

Leaving the wagon at the stable, Pa and Will walked back the way they'd come, down Fifth Street to Division Street. They passed neatly painted storefronts, boardwalks protecting the businesses from street dust. Some stores had chairs and benches sitting beneath shaded verandas. A few saddle horses and a couple of horse-drawn buggies were tied to hitching rails and posts.

The First National Bank was housed on the ground floor of the Scriver building. Two large arched windows stared out on either side of the arched doorway. Pa and Will entered. Inside was cool and quiet, the only sound the ticking of the colonial clock. Will looked up to check the time: one-thirty.

He followed Pa up to the long wooden counter stretching almost the width of the bank. At the left end, it curved and extended the length of the room. The floorboards squeaked as they walked up to the counter. Mr. Bunker, the teller, left his desk to help Pa.

"Come to make a deposit," said Pa. He counted off a number of bills and handed them to Mr. Bunker, who counted them again, aloud. Dipping a quill pen into an ink bottle, Mr. Bunker opened a large ledger and recorded Pa's name, the date, and the amount of the deposit. With a quiet "Thank you," Mr. Bunker carried the money to a large walk-in vault. Inside stood a heavy steel safe, impressive with its bolts and padlocks. There could be a lot of money in there, thought Will. Everyone in town, every farmer, kept savings there. Mr. Bunker put the money inside and shot the bolts across, but he didn't close the time lock.

Mr. Heywood, dressed in a neat black suit and black bow tie, rose from his table in a small open work area.

"Good afternoon, Mr. Sasse," he said, his eyes dark and grave. He came over and shook Pa's hand.

Pa nodded respectfully and Will snatched off his hat. "My wife tells me you'll be raising purebred Belgian horses." He ran his strong hand over his neatly trimmed black beard. "A good business to enter," he observed. "Always an increasing need."

Pa straightened his own tie. "That's what I figured," he said. "Good business prospects. Good money to be made."

Mr. Heywood nodded politely and went back to his desk.

"Pa," whispered Will as they turned to go out, "Mr. Bunker didn't lock the safe. He shut the door and threw the bolts, but it's not locked tight."

Pa stepped outside and pulled the door shut behind them. "I reckon it's safe," he said. "Once the time lock is closed, it can't be opened again till the next morning. So they can't lock it till the end of the day. The money's secure enough in the vault."

Crossing the street to Wheeler's Apothecary, Pa went inside to buy cloves for Ma. Will stood near the bench in front of the apothecary's window where a young man sat watching the bustle on Division Street, his feet up on a porch railing in front of him. The neat white-painted railing made the boardwalk seem like a front porch. The young man smiled and made room for Will.

"Hello, Mr. Wheeler," Will said as he sat down. "Or is it Dr. Wheeler now?"

"Not 'doctor' yet," said Mr. Wheeler. "I'll be going back to medical school again this fall, for my last year. You can still call me Mr. Wheeler. Better yet, call me Henry." He watched the horses, buggies, and wagons passing by, pedestrians walking the boardwalks. "Lots of folks in town today."

"Busy," agreed Will, looking across the square. That was Frank, riding over the bridge into town on his dun-colored gelding, with a stranger riding on each side of him. All wore the long linen dusters. They rode past Will halfway down the street, dismounted, and tied their horses to the hitching rail in front of the bank. But instead of going inside, they walked to the end of the block and sat on some packing boxes in front of Lee & Hitchcock's dry goods store. The two strangers rolled and lit cigarettes. Frank whittled. All three kept looking up and down the street.

They probably have a big horse sale pending. Will watched the street, too, wondering who might be bringing fine horses to town. There came Cole and Clell down Division Street from the opposite direction.

Clell tied his horse to the hitching rail in front of

the bank and stood in front of its door. Still out in the street, Cole got off his horse and raised the stirrup to adjust the saddle girth. Frank and the other two walked down the boardwalk to meet them, tossing cigarettes in the street. Will watched Cole tie his horse to the rail, too, and saw him gazing back the way he'd come. Looking back to the square, Will saw three more horsemen cross the bridge, riding abreast, eyes taking in every person, every movement. Dusters loose about them, they each rode with one hand on his hip, each hat pulled low and tight.

"That's Jesse," Will told Henry. "I guess the others were waiting for him. There must be a big deal in the works. Maybe they're going to buy land, start a cattle ranch."

The hardware store merchant, Mr. Allen, walked briskly up to the bank door. He brushed past Clell, who reached out and grabbed Mr. Allen's arm, pulling him close. Swiftly drawing a pistol, Clell shoved it into Mr. Allen's ribs.

Mr. Allen wrenched free and ran around the corner of the bank to the back alley. Coming out on Mill Square, he hollered loud enough for everyone in town to hear. "Get your guns, boys! They're robbing the bank!"

Will ran out into the street. Frank and Jesse and Cole and the others all had their guns pulled.

"They're outlaws!" yelled Will, shocked.

Henry Wheeler shouted, "Robbery! Robbery!"

Clell and Cole sprang onto the nearest horses, two bays. They charged up and down Division Street.

"Get back!" they yelled at all the startled and confused people who had stopped along the board-walk and in the street. Waving guns and firing in the air as they galloped by, Cole and Clell scattered people and horses in all directions.

Will looked up and saw Cole riding straight down on him.

"Move, kid! Out of the way!" He shot over Will's head. "Get out of here!"

Will leaped back over the railing onto the board-walk. Bullets splintered the door frame above him.

ROBBING THE BANK
Afternoon, September 7, 1876

Whoof. Will's breath was knocked out of him as he hit the boards. Lying flat on the boardwalk, he scrabbled around quickly to see through the porch railing into the street. Dirt clods and dust clouds blinded him. Rearing, neighing, stampeding horses bolted past, dragging buggies and farm wagons with screaming, terrified people desperately hanging on. Will inched back against the storefront and rubbed the dust out of his eyes.

Panicked pedestrians dove into doorways and dashed up side streets, screaming and shouting. Within seconds, the streets cleared of everyone except the robbers. Five charged up and down Division Street, Cole one of them. He was hollering curses, firing shots constantly. Through the rising, roiling dust, Will glimpsed Mr. Bunker running from the alley behind the bank, clutching a bloody shoulder, and yelling "Robbery, robbery!"

Will crept up behind a porch post and pulled himself to his feet, able to see better but not realizing how little protection the narrow post offered. The shooting and shouting brought other people outside to see what was going on. The outlaws rampaging the street fired at them and sent them scurrying as well.

Except for one man. Standing petrified in the center of the street a few feet in front of Will stood a blond young man. A farmer, it looked like. It was the new immigrant from Sweden, Will realized. Looking past him, Will saw an outlaw galloping like the devil toward the young farmer.

"Move! Or I'll kill you!" the gunman shouted, aiming at the terrified man. Will recognized the voice, knew suddenly that the gunman was Cole. Bewildered, frozen in place, the Swedish farmer just stood.

"Get out of the way!" screamed Will, his voice cracking.

The young man turned his head and stared at Will, uncomprehending.

Lightning flashed out of Cole's gun, and the farmer dropped. He lay in the street, not moving.

Blood trickled from his head into the dirt. Cole thundered past, shooting at anything that moved.

Will's heart thudded as loud as the thundering hoofbeats.

Right on the outlaw's heels, the other robbers stormed past, iron-shod hooves throwing great clods of dirt. Will ducked down behind his slender post, gasping for a dusty breath. Through a cloud of whirling dirt and gun smoke, Will made out someone running towards Division Street from Bridge Street. He stood and leaned out to see.

Mr. Allen. It was Mr. Allen, carrying an armful of rifles from his hardware store. Townsfolk materialized around him, grabbing the offered weapons. Mr. Allen yelled something at Mr. Manning. All Will could hear was "—robbing the bank!" but he saw Mr. Manning duck into his hardware store and reach into his window display for a rifle.

They were going to fight back! Will thought of his new rifle.

From behind Will, Henry Wheeler jumped over the porch railing and dashed around the corner of his dad's apothecary, up the alley, and into the back of the Dampier Hotel. Will started to follow Henry, but the steady gunfire and whirlwinds of dust made the street exposed and dangerous.

"For God's sake!" Henry called back to Will, "Stay down!" Will turned back and dived for the boardwalk, flattening as bullets whizzed past his head. Running, even moving, was impossible.

Galloping hooves bore down on him again and he watched though the porch railing. He saw the beautiful buckskin race by. Will strained his eyes through the dust and saw Jesse on the stallion's back, shooting to keep the street clear of people.

A nearby gunshot yanked Will's attention upward, to his left. Will stood again, stepping to his left, one hand still gripping his post. Scanning the Dampier Hotel's second floor, then the third, Will saw Henry poke a rifle out a window, searching for a target from his high vantage point. Will looked back down to the street. An outlaw jerked his horse to a stop in front on the bank. Will strained to see if he knew who it was.

Jumping off his horse, the outlaw ran to the bank door and yelled, "Come out! Come out of there! We have to go!"

As the outlaw raced back to his skittish horse, Mr. Manning stepped out of his store and fired point-blank at the outlaw as he attempted to remount. With one foot on the ground and one foot in the stirrup, the outlaw was jolted back. His foot slipped out of the stirrup and he fell, his horse shying sideways. He managed to hold onto the reins.

Will stared at the familiar face, blood streaming from its scalp. Wounded, Clell pulled his horse to him, grabbed the saddle horn, and mounted.

Will's hand grasped his chest. It felt very tight. It hurt to breathe.

Manning, having loaded his rifle, dashed out onto the street at the corner of the Scriver building. He had a good view of two outlaws who had dismounted in front of the bank, guarding the door. They stood behind their horses, picking their shots.

Will gulped down a deep breath and called to Manning, "They're using their horses for cover! They can shoot everyone from behind their horses!"

Raising his rifle, taking slow and careful aim, Manning deliberately shot one of the horses. It screamed and thudded to the ground. Will stared at the dying horse. He gripped the post for support, his knees weak.

The two outlaws, now exposed, looked around to see where the shot had come from. Will looked back at Manning, who had ducked back around the corner to reload his rifle, and knew that outlaws hadn't figures out who had fired. When Manning stepped out again, he sighted his rifle on one of the outlaws standing between the two remaining horses and the bank door. He fired and again dropped back behind the corner of the building.

His bullet grazed an outside stairway alongside the bank. One of the robbers grabbed his hip, nearly falling. He lurched under the iron stairwell for cover.

Shots came again from Henry Wheeler's third-floor window. Will looked up, then down to see who Henry was firing at. It was Cole.

Cole rode past the Dampier Hotel directly beneath Henry's window. Henry's long rifle barrel followed Cole's movements for a second or two, and then Henry fired. Too high—he missed. Still at a gallop, Cole looked up and spotted Henry. He pointed his revolver at the window and fired back. Jagged shards of glass rained down on the street. The shattered remnants left in the pane quivered. Henry had safely ducked back and quickly reloaded. He leaned out the window again. His rifle barrel followed the next rider, and Henry fired. Accurately.

Clell, face still bleeding, was hit—again. He slumped forward, pitched out of the saddle, and thudded to the dirt. His horse reared and raced away. Clell twitched a few times, then lay still.

Will leaned out past his post, staring at the unmoving body. Clell's outstretched hand still grasped his pistol. Will still heard gunshots, but they sure weren't coming from Clell. Will looked back to Manning, who had reloaded and was surveying the scene. Will followed Manning's glance. A mounted outlaw halfway up the street was scanning windows and storefronts.

"He's covering the bank door," Will shouted. "He fires at anyone who sticks his head out a door or window."

Slowly, taking deliberate aim, Manning fired at this man. The outlaw slammed backward, fell from the saddle to the ground like a sack of grain, and lay face down in the dirt, not moving at all. The panicked horse raced past Will, its hooves scattering dirt and gravel, headed toward the livery stable.

The wounded outlaw crouching under the stairway spotted Manning. Raising his pistol, the man aimed through the iron steps.

"Look out!" Will called to Manning. "Under the stairs!"

Bullets shattered the stone wall next to Manning's head and shards of stone flew into his face. Will flinched and yelped as if the rock had hit his own face. Manning and the outlaw dodged back and forth, firing at each other several times.

Just then, a shot from above—from Henry's hotel window—hit the wounded outlaw who was firing at Manning. Cool as could be, the gunman switched the pistol to his left hand, turned and fired up at Henry, who ducked back inside the hotel room. Manning had also ducked back to reload, and Will saw the wounded gunman slump down under the stairs close against the wall, loading bullets into his revolver.

Running on foot down the center of Division Street, yelling and hollering and firing shotguns, three more outraged men joined the gun battle. Encouraged, storekeepers stepped out of their doors and fired their weapons at the rampaging outlaws. More citizens appeared. Old Mr. Hobbs and Justice Streater came down a side street, weaponless, and began hurling rocks and curses at the outlaws.

"Stone 'em!" called the furious, fearless old gentlemen.

The outlaw still guarding the bank yelled inside

the door, "The game is up! Get out, boys! Now! They're killing all our men!"

Two holdup men the bank rushed out of the bank's door into the street. Skirting the dead horse, they doubled up on one of the two remaining horses. His heart in his throat, Will watched the last outlaw come out of the bank, stop in the doorway, and fire a final shot inside.

Turning to the street again, the man grabbed the nearest horse's reins loose from the hitching rail and sprang up onto a dun-colored horse. The outlaw just ahead of him mounted the buckskin stallion.

The horses reared and wheeled as the bank robbers fought to escape. Gunfire raining on them, they shot back, spurring their horses away.

"Don't leave me here!" screamed the wounded outlaw from under the stairwell.

Cole wheeled his horse around to the steps alongside the bank. He pulled up short and the horse stopped instantly, responding to its expert rider. The wounded outlaw staggered out, heading toward Cole.

Will stepped off the boardwalk into the street.

Cole leaned down, grabbed the man's belt, and hoisted him up behind the saddle. Blood staining his elbow, the wounded robber wrapped his good arm around Cole. A close gunshot blew off Cole's hat as they galloped away.

A gunman returned. Jesse had wheeled his horse around for a final dash down the street. Every gun in town fired at him, but on he came, dodging all bullets. He slowed slightly by Clell and the other robber lying in the street. Will knew Jesse saw the blood, knew he saw that they couldn't be helped or rescued. Jesse veered around the slain horse, now quiet and still, and spurred his mount through a hailstorm of gunfire back the way he had come.

Will stood before him in the street, alone and unprotected. The big stallion galloped headlong at him.

Jesse's eyes met Will's and widened, seeming startled to see him there. Jesse faltered for a split second.

The galloping horse bore down on Will. He couldn't move.

At the last instant before he would have rode Will down, Jesse leaned left, the neck reins swiftly turning the big bucksin, his spurs touching the flanks.

Will felt the whoosh of wind as the horse raced past him. Smelled sweaty horse and damp saddle leather and blood. Words and images pinged around the inside of Will's skull like bullets ricocheting around him. *"A man's got to go after what he wants. Got good secure banks in your town?"*

With a burst of speed, Jesse followed the gang out of town. A great whirling flurry of dust obscured their escape.

Will choked and coughed. He clasped his hands over his eyes, but still he saw the flash and flare of gunfire. Gunshots rang in his ears and inside his head.

MR. HEYWOOD STOOD FIRM
Afternoon, September 7, 1876

Coughing and gasping on the choking dust, Will stepped back onto the boardwalk and leaned against the apothecary storefront. He rubbed his eyes, surprised to find his face wet and gritty. Dimly, he was aware of people running past him, of shouting, of distant gunfire, of clanging school and church bells.

"Will! You're all right!"

Strong arms covered with rough wool wrapped around Will's neck, the smell of tobacco surrounded him. His breathing calmed, his heartbeat slowed, and he hugged Pa back.

"Are you safe, Pa? You're not hurt?" Will's shaky voice was muffled in Pa's sleeve.

Pa stepped back and looked Will up and down. His voice was a bit shaky, too. "No, son. Not hurt.

The gunfire pinned us down, but we weren't hit."

Pa turned his head and gestured at the storefront. It was riddled with bullet holes. Splinters were hanging from shredded boards. The window to the left of the door was shattered.

Will hadn't heard glass breaking behind him.

Henry Wheeler ran toward them. "Will! Mr. Sasse! Is your rig handy?"

"Just up the street at the livery stable," answered Pa. "Still hitched up."

"A wagon?" Will asked, then looked around, shuddering when he saw bodies in the street. He couldn't take his eyes off a slow spreading bloodstain next to the farmer.

"We need to get the wounded over to Dr. Coons," called Henry, running into the street. He rolled the farmer over and put his head to his chest, listening for a heartbeat. "He's still alive!"

Pa slapped Will on the back. "Folks need our help, Will. Jump to it."

Will ran down Fifth Street to the livery, glad to be moving, to be doing something. Within two minutes, he reached the stable and untied Penny and Pete. They snorted and pranced, still unnerved from all the gunfire. Will climbed into the buckboard and slapped the reins on the horse's rumps, but they needed no urging and cantered quickly back to Mill Square.

Pa and Henry carefully lifted the young farmer onto the wagon box as Will dropped the end gate. Mr. Bunker, holding his bleeding shoulder, lurched up to the wagon.

"Going to Doc Coons?" he asked, his face white, his eyes glassy. Onlookers gathered around, peppering them with questions.

Will helped Mr. Bunker to a seated position on the tailgate, letting his legs dangle off the end of the wagon. Pa sat beside him, steadying him. Will drove quickly.

As Dr. Coons attended the farmer in the dispensary, Henry and Will helped Mr. Bunker onto a tall stool in Dr. Coon's outer office. Pa returned to the Square to see if anyone else needed him.

Deftly cutting away Mr. Bunker's bloody shirt, Henry motioned toward the hanging cupboard.

"Should be a basin in there, Will. Fetch some hot water and soap."

Will quickly found the white enamel basin and ran to the kitchen. He returned with an armful of clean towels.

"Mrs. Coons will be right here with hot water. She was heating some for Dr. Coons, too." He pulled a stool alongside Mr. Bunker.

Henry inspected the bullet wound, front and back. "You're a lucky man, Alonzo," he said. "The bullet went clean through without nicking a bone or an artery." He reached for a towel, applying pressure to stop the bleeding. Mrs. Coons bustled through with two steaming basins, set one next to Henry, and went without a word into the dispensary.

"What happened in the bank, Mr. Bunker?" asked Will, aware that talking would distract the teller from Henry's probing.

Mr. Bunker stared at the wall as if he was still inside the bank, seeing everything happen again.

"I was working at my ledgers when I heard the door open," he began. "I thought it was a customer and went to the counter." His voice became strident. "Three men charged in, waving big pistols, two apiece! 'We're holding up the bank!' they yelled. 'Don't holler or we'll shoot you! Got forty men outside!'" Mr. Bunker waved his good arm, gesturing at things only he could see.

Henry put his hand on Alonzo's good shoulder. "Don't move, Alonzo. Tell us slow-like."

The teller took a long deep breath, unaware of what Henry was doing to his wounded shoulder, and looked straight at Will. "They jumped clean over the counter, shouting in my face. 'Who's the cashier?' they demanded. Of course we're all scared. We all said we weren't the cashier. That the cashier wasn't here today. Then they grabbed Mr. Heywood by the shirt, slapped him around, and shoved him against the wall."

Mr. Bunker, his eyes very wide, gulped a few breaths. "They wanted Mr. Heywood to open the safe, but he refused. He said the time lock was on and it couldn't be opened. That made them so mad they pistol-whipped him. Nearly knocked him unconscious."

Will frowned slightly and pursed his lips, remembering the unbolted time lock.

Mr. Bunker's voice was getting screechy. "They jammed their guns in my face, and in Mr. Wilcox's, too. 'Open that safe!' they hollered, swearing and cursing something fierce. We were plenty scared, but insisted we couldn't open it."

Mr. Bunker stopped talking, eyes gone blank. Henry opened a bottle of iodine. A strong, bitter odor filled the air.

Giving his head a slight shake, Mr. Bunker continued. "Guess that was the truth. We couldn't unlock it because it was already unlocked!" He chuckled, his voice squeaking at the same time. "The bolts were in place, but not locked."

"Did they find out?" Will asked, leaning forward and putting his hand on Mr. Bunker's good arm.

The slight grin that had been on Mr. Bunker's face slid off it. "They sure were angry! They shoved Mr. Wilcox and me down on the floor. Started beating Mr. Heywood again. They threatened to cut his throat if he wouldn't open the safe. One of them drew a big knife across his throat, just enough to draw blood!" He gasped as Henry swabbed his wound with the iodine.

"Then what happened?" Will quickly prompted.

"Mr. Heywood stood firm! Brave, brave man," gasped Mr. Bunker. "While I was on the floor," he continued, "I tried to reach for a small derringer we keep under the counter. But I was spotted. An outlaw saw me reaching for it and grabbed it away from me and shoved me down on the floor again. Lucky for me he was more interested in rummaging through the drawers looking for money than in beating me."

A tight smile flitted across Alonzo Bunker's face. "I showed him where the petty cash was kept and he stuffed about twelve dollars into a grain sack." His smile widened a bit. "I don't believe he ever found the three thousand dollars in the counter box." He winced as Henry wound the gauze tightly around his wound.

"We heard shots from the bank, Mr. Bunker. How were you shot?" asked Will.

Mrs. Coons walked through the room again, this time with a tray of steaming coffee cups. Mr. Bunker took one gratefully and drank a long swallow. He set down the cup and looked at Will.

"When Mr. Heywood kept refusing to open the safe for them, they slammed him against the wall and fired a pistol right next to his face, I suppose to scare him more. That's when I made a dash for the back door. I shoved my way through the door just as a bullet shattered one of the window blinds right alongside my head."

His voice rose up a screechy notch. "I fell out into the alley, ran down the back steps, and took off running. Their second shot went through my shoulder, but I made it around the corner—" He looked down at his neatly bandaged wound, then smiled at Henry Wheeler. "Nice work, Henry. Good as Doc Coons would have done."

Henry smiled, glancing at Will.

"A little distraction helps."

Dr. Coons came out of the dispensary, wiping

his hands on a towel. At the same time, the front door opened and Mr. Manning and Mr. Allen stepped inside.

"How's that young Swede?" Mr. Manning asked, closing the door gently behind him.

Dr. Coons shook his head. "Doesn't look good. Head wound." He tossed his towel on a chair. "Are there any more wounded?"

Mr. Manning looked at the others in the room.

"Not wounded," he said. "Mr. Heywood is dead. The last robber going out of the bank door turned and fired point-blank at him. Murder, plain and simple."

Will's throat tightened as he thought of the dignified banker. He heard Mr. Bunker's sharp intake of breath.

"Two of the outlaws are dead in the street," Mr. Allen said to Dr. Coons. "We thought you should check them out."

"What about Mr. Heywood?" Will asked. "Where did they take him?"

"Your pa has taken his body to the Heywoods home," said Mr. Allen, sighing deeply. "Their friend from the college, President Strong, went along to break the news to Mrs. Heywood."

Will looked to Mr. Manning. "What happens

next?" Will asked.

"The sheriff's already organizing a posse," said Mr. Manning. "He's telegraphing ahead to neighboring towns." He wiped his face with his clean white handkerchief, looking surprised when it came away so dirty.

"It's just a matter of time before we catch the murdering scoundrels," growled Mr. Allen.

"What about the money in the bank?" asked Mr. Bunker. "Did they finally get it?"

Each man shook his head. No one knew.

PA WAS RIGHT
Evening, September 7, 1876

The horse's heads were barely visible in the darkness. Their clip-clopping hooves combined with the sound of late-season crickets to create a somber sound that echoed Will's mood.

Pa slumped down in the wagon seat, one booted foot on the front boards for support, an occasional whiff of pipe smoke the only sign he was awake.

Will stared blankly ahead. He remembered the times he and Jesse had talked. Jesse had never yelled at him, had never told him what to do. Jesse had listened whenever Will had talked about Star and the kind of horses he hoped to raise. Jesse had liked Star, had admired her. He had let his stallion breed her and hadn't asked for any stud fee. He hadn't seemed mean or greedy.

Will tapped the reins across Pete's and Penny's backs to keep them moving briskly. It was starting to get cold. Fog had settled into pockets in the lowlands. Cold, damp air settled around him and he shivered slightly.

Letting his thoughts run back to the day he first saw Jesse, he searched his mind for any strangeness he should have picked up on. Frank and Jesse had asked about Northfield and the bank and remarked on all the money changing hands. That had seemed normal enough. But then during the supper at their farm, they had asked about the bank again, about how safe it was, how secure. And all Will had thought about was the buckskin stallion and getting his mare bred.

"They would never have come to Northfield if I hadn't invited them!" he blurted out.

"What? Who?" asked Pa, sitting up to stare at Will.

Glancing into Pa's face, Will felt his stomach cramp, his muscles go weak. He stared ahead into the inky darkness.

"Jesse and Frank," he said, his voice very low. "I talked to them at the horse auction. I told them about Star." Will swallowed hard around the lump in his throat. "I told them where we lived. I told them to come by."

"Why'd you do that?" barked Pa, glaring at him.

Will gulped again, feeling guilt settle on his shoulders, heavy as a winter quilt. "I had hoped Jesse's stallion would breed Star," he mumbled.

"And did he?" Pa demanded.

"Think so," Will whispered hoarsely.

"Dang fool boy!" Pa's angry voice startled the horses and the wagon lurched briefly. "You ain't got any more sense than God gave a fence post!"

Grim heavy silence enveloped them the rest of the way home. Will knew that this time Pa was right.

Eventually they drove into their long dirt driveway. Will pulled up alongside the front porch. Ma hurried out the door, the lamplight from the kitchen spilling out around her.

"What happened? Why are you so late?" Her voice was a pitch higher than usual, her words spoken quickly. "I heard the church bells. Was there a fire? A mill accident?"

Pa jumped down from the wagon and brushed past Ma. "Nope. Bank raid," he growled, letting the door slam shut behind him.

Ma turned to Will, her eyes wide. "But what happened? Was anyone hurt?"

With a long deep sigh, Will got down and led the horses toward the barn. Ma walked beside him.

"Remember the cattle buyers that stopped to eat here a week or so ago?" Will asked. "Turns out they were outlaws. They held up the bank this afternoon." He stopped to lift the latch on the barn door. "Mr. Heywood was killed and Mr. Bunker was wounded."

Ma gasped, raising her hands to her mouth.

Will pulled the door open, the hinges protesting with a louder-than-usual screech. "That young Swedish farmer was shot. Also two of the outlaws."

Reaching inside the door, Will took down a lantern that hung on a long nail beside the doorway. Ma silently lifted its chimney and Will struck a wooden match and lit the wick, sending up a brief whiff of sulfur and kerosene. Soft yellow light pushed the darkness back into the corners of the barn. Molly and Mae stirred, nickering softly. Quickly unfastening Pete's and Penny's traces, he led them to their stalls.

Instead of Star's welcoming nicker, Will heard heavy raspy breathing coming from her stall.

Quickly he raised the lantern higher and moved to her stall.

Head down, flanks covered with dried lather, nostrils and mouth still frothy, stood the buckskin stallion. A trickle of blood trailed down from his withers.

Star was gone. The filly huddled in a corner of the stall.

"No!" cried Will. The lantern shook in his outstretched hand and Ma quickly took it from him. He felt her tight grasp on his arm. Star was gone.

DUTY
Late evening, September 7, 1876

"Good old Pete. No wonder Pa thinks so much of you," murmured Will, patting the horse's heavy neck. Head down, plodding along back to Northfield, Pete flicked his ears backward to catch Will's voice.

Straddling Pete's wide bare back, slumped forward because he was so tired, Will thought he had been a fool to think Jesse gave half a hoot about him and his plans. The outlaws had probably planned to steal Star all along. Will twined his fingers in Pete's mane, staring into the dark nothingness ahead. He had never dreamed of causing any harm. Pa was right. Will didn't think.

Pete made a whiffing noise, sounding for all the world as if he was making conversation.

The only thing Will could do now was to let

the sheriff know what direction the outlaws had headed. He thought about Star and a sharp pang ate at his stomach. Even if he didn't get Star back, he hoped she'd be all right. At least Jesse took good care of his horses.

Pete's ears pricked forward as they approached Northfield. A great many lanterns lit up the houses and the streets. As Will crossed the Cannon River Bridge, his curiosity was caught by the crowds of people in Mill Square and on Division Street.

Pete plodded through the crowd, paying no mind to the noise and bustle, but Will tried to pick up on bits of conversation from the people they passed. Witnesses jabbered their version of the events to anyone who would listen, though it seemed to Will that everyone was talking and no one was listening. People stood in small groups, arguing, gesturing, and speculating. No one paid any notice to the boy on the big workhorse.

Mayor Stewart, though, standing in front of his office, saw Will approach and recognized him. The mayor motioned Will over and watched him tie Pete to the hitching post and slide off the horse's broad back. "So, Will," the mayor said. "Why are you back? Something happen?"

Will looked at the two gentlemen standing

beside the mayor and hesitated.

"You know Sheriff Barton and Mr. John Ames," prompted the mayor. "Tell us what you came for." Will held his hat in his hands, twisting its brim.

"Yes sir," he said. "I came to report that the robbers headed west on the Dundas road. They stopped at our place long enough to steal my mare." Will looked down at his dusty boots. "They must have been quick. And quiet. My ma never heard nor saw them." Gazing away down the noisy street, he added, "Their tracks were headed toward Millersberg."

"Valuable information, son," said Sheriff Barton. "We've already sent scouts in just about every direction, every road leading out of town. And telegraphed every station within fifty miles." He stroked his long handlebar mustache. "Sorry about your mare."

Will nodded, looking down the street, not quite able to say anything more.

The sheriff followed his gaze. "Folks have come from miles around to see the dead robbers. Everyone's trying to figure out who they were."

Mr. Ames pointed out a merchant across the street. "Cal Peterman over there claims that one of them is his brother-in-law. Name of Bill Stiles."

Will bit his lip. "I think I know the other one. Only his first name, though."

The three men looked at Will curiously. "Who, do you think?" asked the sheriff.

"His name was Clell. He and three others, named Frank, Jesse, and Cole, stopped at our farm about a week ago." Will's voice was emotionless.

A deep frown creased Sheriff Barton's face. "Frank? Jesse?" he repeated. All three men exchanged knowing, worried looks. The sheriff turned and ran down the boardwalk toward the telegraph office.

Realizing that his information had caused a stir, Will said, "We didn't know..."

Mayor Stewart put a hand on Will's shoulder. "No one knew," he said in a firm voice. "Lots of folks saw them and talked with them. But no one suspected anything like this would happen."

A noisy argument had broken out around the old granary near the livery stable. "What's going on down there?" Will asked.

"We took the dead outlaws to the granary," said the mayor. "They're laid out there on the floor. Everyone wants a close look." A grim smile played across his face. "Maybe someone will be able to positively identify them."

Sheriff Barton returned and said, "I notified the governor. We'll have a posse leaving at first light. Any able-bodied man with a horse and a gun is welcome to join it."

Will looked up at him. "Can I go?"

The sheriff looked at Pete, head low and dozing. "Got a faster horse than that?" he asked with a teasing grin.

"Yes sir. I'll find one. I'll be here," Will said. This time he would do things right. He would use his head.

Slipping his suspenders up over his shoulders, Will peered down the dark, narrow stairwell. He stepped down carefully, keeping to the outside edge of the creaky boards. At the bottom step, he sat and pulled on his boots, lacing the rawhide strings carefully. He would leave a note telling his parents he had gone to join the posse.

Bedsprings creaked and heavy footsteps thudded above Will. He should have known he couldn't get past Pa, Will thought. Shoulders sagging, he went into the kitchen. Pa came down as Will was lighting the lantern. Light steps followed. Ma didn't sleep through anything either.

"Thinking of going back to Northfield?" asked Pa. He sat on a kitchen chair and pulled on his own boots. Ma stoked the coals in the cookstove and added dry kindling. The gray enamel coffeepot on the back of the stove was full of water, ready to heat. Will set out plates and cups.

"Yes sir," he said quietly. "Sheriff Barton's sending out the posse at first light. I though I'd go with them."

"Where in tarnation did you get that fool idea?" growled Pa. "No sense to it at all." The rooster crowing broke the silence that followed.

"The robbery wouldn't have happened at all if it weren't for me," Will muttered. "Telling them about Star is what brought the outlaws this way."

"You didn't know they were outlaws," argued Pa. "We didn't know it when they sat around our table. Wasn't no more your fault than ours."

"Pa, it was my fault," insisted Will. "Folks are dead because of me. I've got to make it right. Only makes sense, doesn't it, Pa? I've got to set it right." Ma turned from the stove.

"It's too dangerous for the boy," she said, a slight catch in her throat. Bacon sizzled behind her in the cast-iron skillet. Pa turned his back and pumped a basin full of wash water at the dry sink. He didn't say anything for awhile, then muttered, "The boy's right. He's got a duty."

No one spoke. It got so quiet Will thought the bacon might stop sizzling, too. Then Pa added, in a firmer voice, "Don't worry none. He'll be fine. There'll be plenty of good men going along."

Ma added fresh grounds to the boiling pot and the delicious aroma of hot coffee drifted through the chilly kitchen.

"The outlaws know Will and us. They know where we live." Her voice had a slight tremor. "What if they come back here? What if they think we gave the posse information?"

"Nothing will happen here that I can't handle," Pa said sharply. He turned to Will. "You go with the posse. Do what needs doing." He opened the back door. "I'll saddle the stallion. He's ready to ride again. Pack a bedroll. You might be gone a few days." The door slammed behind him.

Ma stood with her back to the stove, looking from the door to Will. The bacon began to smoke and burn.

Will got his saddlebags off a hook by the back door and began stuffing them with a change of clothes that lay neatly folded in the laundry basket.

He didn't look at Ma, but he knew that her face looked real scared.

"We'll capture those outlaws in no time, Ma. They're all shot up already. Probably there's no fight left in them." Will talked fast and moved fast. Ready to leave, he hugged Ma tightly.

"Take care. God keep you safe," Ma whispered. She filled a heavy white flour sack. "Bread and sausage and apples. And here's bacon and bread to eat now, while you ride. And take your heavy jacket. It's going to rain."

Pa stood outside, holding the stallion. He gave Will a leg up on the tall horse.

"See you soon, Pa," Will said.

Pa nodded but said nothing. He slapped the horse's rump and Will galloped away. The rising sun struggled to send a few rays through dark blue clouds on the eastern horizon. The fresh morning air had a damp chill.

Scarcely an hour later, Will trotted up to Manning's Hardware. Several horses were tied to the hitching rail, heads down in a cold drizzling rain. He reined the stallion into the alleyway, hoping for a little shelter from the wind. Dismounting, Will patted the horse's neck. Its head was held high, ears flicking back and forth.

"You remember this place from yesterday, don't you, boy?" Will said. He pushed his own memories of the day before, and of Star, out of his mind.

Will checked the saddle girth. Star's saddle sat high on the stallion's back, the cinch pulled to the ends of the straps but holding. Will ran his fingers under the bridle, letting the reins fall to the ground. With all the straps let out to the last buckle hole, it seemed to be a comfortable fit.

The stallion shook his head suddenly, jangling the bridle and splashing raindrops like a dog shaking itself dry. Will smiled a tight, tense smile.

"We're in for a cold, wet ride, Buck," he said. Will didn't know what Jesse had named the horse, but Pa had called him Buck a few times the previous night as they were grooming him. The new name came naturally to Will.

Noticing the horse had not moved since he had dismounted, Will whistled softly.

"You're trained to stay where your reins are dropped, aren't you, Buck?" The stallion shook his head up and down as if he agreed with Will.

Will stepped onto the boardwalk, brushing

rainwater off his long jacket and wide-brimmed hat. Opening the door, he saw a group of men talking loudly by the gun case. Mr. Manning, looking somewhat harried, glanced over at the door and smiled at Will.

"Will, lad." he said. Leaving his customers, Mr. Manning waved Will over to the wide oak counter. A tall, shiny cash register stood on one end of the counter. A wide roll of brown wrapping paper and a ball of string were on metal attachments at the other end. Mr. Manning stood in the middle, hands spread on the polished oak countertop.

"Have you still got my rifle, Mr. Manning?" Will asked. "You haven't sold it, have you?"

"Of course not," said Mr. Manning, bending down to reach under the counter. He brought up the fine rifle Pa had chosen. "It's yours. Bought and paid for. I added an artillery strap so you can sling it over your shoulder when you're riding." He clapped a box of ammunition on the counter.

Will hesitated, wondering if bullets were included in the deal.

"Bought and paid for," Manning repeated. Glancing at the customers at the gun case, Manning raised his voice a notch. "I expect you're joining the posse, Will. They're forming up at the hotel. I'll be closing shop in fifteen minutes. See you there."

Will put on his hat and reached for his gun.

"See you there," Will echoed Mr. Manning.

Trying to ignore the cold drizzle, Will rode Buck onto Division Street. He was surprised at the size of the crowd milling about. Had to be hundreds of people.

The sheriff had set up temporary headquarters in the Dampier Hotel. Sitting atop the tall stallion, Will observed the sheriff and his deputies registering the posse volunteers. Five or six men were gathered together, spoken to, and sent out of town one group after another.

Henry Wheeler, riding a large black gelding, sidled up beside Will. He grinned at Will and appraised the buckskin. "'Morning, Will. I hear you've traded horses, albeit unknowing and unwilling."

Will shrugged. "I'm afraid so, Henry." Not wanting to talk about it, he pointed to the sheriff. "What's going on?"

"They're assigning picket duty," answered Henry, adjusting a poncho over his wet shoulders. "The sheriff hopes to cut off the outlaw's escape by posting pickets at every crossroads, bridge, and ford." He laughed, rueful. "He hopes that will get some of these clumsy reward seekers out of his way."

Will looked at Henry. "Reward?"

A few drops fell off the brim of Henry's hat as he nodded.

"Yeah. The bank offered a reward. So did the governor. Not to mention the previous ones offered by the railroad companies."

Will frowned. "Previous rewards? For what? Who for?"

Henry stared at Will. "Haven't you heard? The outlaws are thought to be Frank and Jesse James and the Younger brothers. The James-Younger gang has been holding up banks and trains in Missouri ever since the Civil War ended. They're a notorious outlaw gang."

Stunned, Will asked, "Why did they come to Minnesota?"

"Who knows? Probably got too hot for them in Missouri." Henry shrugged.

Clang! Clang! Clang! Mr. Ames had come out of the hotel and started banging on the wrought-iron dinner bell under the porch roof, out of the cold drizzling rain. Having gotten the crowd's attention, he called off lists of names, appointing posse members to various local and state law officers.

"Ames is setting up the tracking parties," explained Manning, riding up alongside them. He was wearing a long leather coat to keep the rain off.

"Sheriff Barton's over there," he said, pointing down the street. "We'll ride with him." Will was glad to hear that. He didn't want to trail behind a group of strangers. Mr. Ames clanged the bell again, keeping the noisy chatter down.

"Our scouts report the outlaws were seen at Dundas and at Millersberg. They're riding fast and hard. When their horses are worn out, they steal others. They're leaving quite a trail of spent horses." Mr. Ames sounded as if he was scolding the crowd for the robber's misdeeds. But it was good news to Will.

"Maybe Star will be found. Maybe she'll be left at another farm," he said.

"Could be," Manning said. He chuckled a bit. "The outlaws didn't steal every horse they came across, though. Bill Morris and his bride had just left the church in their surrey when the bank robbers stopped them and demanded their horse. Bill's new wife got all tearful and said they'd just come from their wedding and having their only good horse stolen weren't no way to start a marriage.

Bill told me the leader, probably Jesse James, laughed, tipped his hat to the bride, and said he'd find himself another horse farther on. Bill said no one believed him. No one thought an outlaw would be so gentlemanly."

Mr. Ames's booming voice continued, "The outlaws were last seen at Shieldsville. A posse from Faribault exchanged shots with the dastardly criminals, who unfortunately escaped into the woods." Cheers and jeers went up from the crowd.

Manning shook his head at the unruly onlookers. "Too many of these so-called posse members think this is all a wild adventure and that they'll get rich quick. It will be interesting to see how long they last in the woods and marshes in this cold rain."

Will pulled his hat down firmly, glad it was wide enough to keep the rain off his neck. He would last as long as it took. And until he got Star back.

The posses dispersed, riding off in different directions. Will, Henry, and Manning joined Sheriff Barton and headed out toward Waterville. The streets of Northfield had turned to thick wet mud, pockmarked and puddled by a great many hoofprints.

Riding past the First National Bank, Will

couldn't help but look over. Rivulets of rainwater streaked down the windows. The interior was dark and empty. A hand-scrawled sign, "Closed for funeral," hung crookedly on the doorknob.

Will shivered, the chill running down his back not entirely caused by the cold rain.

THE POSSE
Monday, September 11, 1876

Will looked out the door of the stone barn where
their posse had spent the night. It was just coming
dawn, cold and misty. The relentless rain dripped
off the eaves, splattering into muddy puddles. It
hadn't let up in three days.

Everything connected with this pursuit had
been miserable. The outlaws, avoiding main roads,
had taken to the thick woods. The area south and
west of Northfield was a vast tract of forest. Low-
lying swamps and marshes scattered between steep
hills created a terrain that made progress difficult.
The steady rain drenched the ground and the
trees, swelling rivers and streams. Tracking was
next to impossible, and they hadn't gotten very far
beyond Northfield.

Pungent steam rose off the horses as the men

saddled them. Will picked up his damp blanket, rolled it and used rawhide strips to tie it behind his saddle. Buck's head was down to nose through the straw for any overlooked oats.

"Haven't seen hide nor hair of those outlaws," Will muttered to Buck. He pulled the cinch tight. "This has all been a big waste of time."

The door banged open as the farmer came in carrying a steaming pot of coffee and a basket covered with a striped dish towel.

"Good morning," he said. "The missus knows you can't stay for breakfast, but she said you'd need biscuits and sidepork and hot coffee."

Will's mouth watered at the wonderful warm smells released when the farmer lifted off the towel. Rations had been pretty skimpy the last few days. The steaming hot coffee warmed Will's bones and the tin cup warmed his hands. He reached for a hot baking-powder biscuit. The farmwife had been generous with the butter. Just like Ma.

Sitting on a straw bale, Will carefully balanced his tin cup and biscuits. Henry sat across from him on a nail keg. Henry watched Buck nosing Will for one of the biscuits and laughed. "How's your new horse working out? Looks right friendly."

Will elbowed Buck backwards. "He's really nice, but I sure want to get Star back. She's my brood mare. I already have a nice little filly from her."

The farmer stood in the doorway, watching the raindrops like he was counting them. "Over yonder," he said, "my neighbor Quiram said his dogs set up a ruckus about three nights ago. I wouldn't rightly know if strangers were passing by or whether the hounds had just treed a raccoon."

Sheriff Barton walked up to the door and looked out. Beyond lay steep, wooded hills with a narrow road carved through ravines and hollows.

"We might as well check it out," he said. "We don't have any other leads."

The farmer, chewing on a long piece of straw, nodded. "Lives just past the Bell church. Big curve in the road."

The men mounted up, pulled their hats down low and rode off into the chilling drizzle. Will hunched his shoulders, glad the wind was at his back.

"I'm glad we had food and shelter overnight," said Henry. "I reckon the outlaws are suffering from exposure, what with most of them wounded." A frown rippled his brow. He reached down to his doctor's bag, hanging from a saddle strap, as if to reassure himself it was still there.

After an hour's ride, up and over and down hills, under dripping overhanging branches, they neared Farmer Quiram's barnyard. Three hound dogs bounded toward them, barking and yelping and jumping straight up in the air. A tall, wiry farmer in high-backed overalls called them off.

"You're the posse, I reckon," he said, eyeing Sheriff Barton's badge. "Your best bet is to follow yon creek to German Lake. Want to take the hounds with you?"

The sheriff was pulling hard on the reins of his horse, which was dodging the bounding dogs. "No thanks," he said. "Just point us in the right direction."

Farmer Quiram did just that, wordlessly. Will looked ahead where he pointed. All sloughs and marshes. Frogs croaking, red-winged blackbirds cawing. Probably full of snakes and muskrats.

"Leastwise we're out of the woods with those everlasting brambles and raspberry thickets," grumbled Manning. They set off at a trot, making time before the road became trail, and trail became path, and path became swamp grass and cattails, which happened a lot sooner than anyone wanted.

Chilled and discouraged, Will rode behind the

others. Icy water splashed up on his legs as Buck charged through a running stream. Will thought this was nothing but a wild goose chase. Who could know if this is where the farmer's dogs had gone three nights ago? And chasing what? Raccoons, probably.

"It's as if the swamp swallowed them up," said Henry, dropping back to ride beside Will. "We might as well give up and go home."

Suddenly, Buck's ears pricked forward and his head went up. He flared his nostrils with a snort, then a whinny and broke into a canter.

"Give him his head, Will," called the sheriff, pulling his horse out of the way to let Buck by.

Buck headed for a thick grove of willow trees, thick as a solid wall. Will heard neighing in there. It sounded like several horses. His heart quickened. Maybe Star. . . .

Buck found a break in the slender trunks and pushed through. Will lowered himself to Buck's neck to dodge the whippy branches. Breaking through into a clearing, Will looked around. There were the horses. Two bays and a black.

Not Star.

It was an abandoned campsite. The sheriff, Henry, and Manning followed Will through the break in the trees that Buck had found. They all dismounted and looked around. Saw nothing left but trampled grass and a long dead campfire.

"The horses have been here quite a spell," noted Henry. "All the grass within their reach is grazed clean. Even the leaves are eaten off the branches."

"They've been gone for days," said Sheriff Barton. "They must have gone on foot to avoid being tracked, while all our posses have been struggling on horseback through hills and woods and swamps. Now the outlaws have a three-day lead on all of us." He kicked the wet ashes of the campfire in disgust. "We might as well take their horses back to Northfield. Nothing to see here. The rain washed away any tracks they might have left."

Will knew his hopes of ever seeing Star again were trickling away, too. He got back on Buck, taking the lead rope of one of the stranded horses. Back out of the willow thicket, he rode up alongside the sheriff. "What should I do with Buck, here? Will you want to take him back?"

"As far as I'm concerned," said the sheriff, "you can keep him till the rightful owner claims him. But I want to be there when that happens!" They all laughed, even Will.

Dropping back to ride beside Henry, Will realized the sheriff had just told him Buck was his to keep. This fine stallion was now his, a great addition to his breeding stock. He still had the filly, which in a couple of years would be a brood mare.

Henry interrupted his thoughts. "What did your Pa think of the James boys when they stopped at your farm?" he asked. "Did he have any suspicions?"

"No," said Will. "He thought, like me, that they were fine fellows. Especially when they paid him cash for the meal."

"Did they, now?" mused Henry. "Paid their bills up front? Your pa probably wouldn't even have asked them to pay. Giving them a meal was just being neighborly."

Will frowned without realizing it as he puzzled over the strange nature of the outlaws. Sometimes the outlaws did some decent things. Jesse had stolen Star, but left the buckskin in Star's stall, probably because he knew Will would care for him. Maybe even as a trade—Buck in exchange for Star. And Jesse'd let the newlyweds keep their horse even when he was running for his life. Then the outlaws did terrible things, robbed banks and trains. Will'd seen a man shoot Mr. Heywood—had seen Cole

kill that innocent farmer in the street.

Returning to Northfield, which took a lot less time when the posse could go on roads and not cross-country, they found the streets still full of milling noisy people, probably posses that had also returned empty-handed. The sight of Sheriff Barton's posse, which led the string of recovered horses but no captured outlaws, quickly drew a group around them. The sheriff inched his group through the crowd to the hotel. He directed a deputy to take the extra horses to Faribault, the county seat.

They dismounted and tied their horses and went up onto the hotel veranda. The people, still crowded around them, shouted questions. "Where'd you find the horses? Are they the outlaw's horses? Any sign of Jesse James? Where'd they go?"

Sheriff Barton turned to the crowd, motioning them to move back.

"We found the horses at an abandoned campsite near German Lake. Who knows where the James Gang is by now?" he growled. He went inside the hotel to his office and slammed the door behind him.

The crowd soon dispersed, leaving Henry,

Manning, and Will standing under the veranda roof, watching the cold drizzle turn to steady rain. Soon the street was an empty muddy quagmire. Gray rain streamed off the overhang, ran in streams down gray downspouts, washed down gray windows, and gathered into great gray puddles.

"At least the robbers haven't come back to take vengeance on the townsfolk," said Manning.

"Can't see that they'd want to come back here for anything," said Henry.

"They'll be spotted again," Manning said with no assurance in his voice whatsoever. "They can't have gotten too far on foot, without food or medical help. We'll be riding again soon." Water ran off his hat's brim as he nodded. "Keep checking with us, Will. Maybe some new leads will come in."

They walked off the porch and mounted their horses, mud on their boots clogging up the stirrups. Soaking wet and chilled to the bone, they rode off to their respective homes in hopes of a warm bath, dry clothing, and a hot meal.

A pale sun struggled through ragged rain clouds, but a dark, damp mist settled around and in Will as he plodded home.

RIDING LIKE THE DEVIL
Wednesday, September 13, 1876

The first rosy streaks of dawn reflected off low-lying banks of mist hovering over the meadow pasture. A burnished red rooster strutted out of the henhouse, leaped onto the rail fence, flapped his wings, stretched out full length, and crowed "Er-er-er-roo! Er-er-er-roo!" Shaking his shining feathers back into place, the rooster leaped down to await his reward of ground corn and millet.

Will came out a side door of the barn and loosed the cows to pasture, giving each a pat on the rump as it ambled past him. Pa walked out the barnyard-side door carrying two milk cans to the cool springhouse. Fragrant wood smoke drifted out of the chimney of the house. Freshly brewed egg-coffee would be waiting in the kitchen. A week after the devastating bank robbery, life had returned to its normal routine.

Thundering hoofbeats drowned out the gentle morning birdsong as three horsemen galloped into the barnyard. Squawking, fluttering, and flapping, the rooster and his hen harem scattered every which way.

"Will!" called Sheriff Barton as he, Henry, and Manning pulled their horses to a clattering stop. "The outlaws have been sighted near Mankato. Crossed the Blue Earth River over the railroad trestle." Catching his breath, he took off his hat and beat it against his leg, shaking off trail dust. He put it back on nice and straight, then brushed his unruly mustache back to handsome and rubbed the dust off his badge.

Will ran toward the horsemen, but Pa caught his arm.

"I'll get Buck saddled. You get your gear. Tell Ma you'll be leaving," Pa said and hurried back into the barn.

"Be right with you," Will called to the sheriff. Heart pounding in his chest, he raced into the house for his riding boots and extra clothes. Within minutes he joined Pa in the barn and tied his saddlebags and bedroll behind Buck's saddle.

Pa had also secured a bag of oats there. "You'll

have to keep Buck fed. You'll be riding him pretty hard." He double-checked the straps and buckles. "Have better luck this time. Look sharp, now."

"I will, Pa," Will said. "We'll get it done. And I'll get Star back, too."

Pa reached for Buck's reins and led him outside. "I hope this doesn't take much longer. It's nearly time to start harvest. We've got a lot of work ahead of us."

Will looked at the long corn rows in the field across the road, the ears hanging heavy. "Hard work will get it done," he said. "I'll be back soon."

Ma met them at the front step and gave Will a flour sack. "Apples, cheese, and biscuits," she said. "Do you want some tomatoes from the garden?"

"Ma," Will said, "I can't carry a sack of tomatoes on horseback." Somewhat embarrassed, he glanced at the men waiting for him. They looked like they would have liked some fresh tomatoes.

"Yes, you're right," said Ma. She hugged him and gave him a kiss on his cheek.

"Come back safe," she whispered, eyes grave and full of worry.

He hugged her back and said, "Surely will, Ma." He mounted Buck and joined the others, who already had turned their horses, anxious to leave.

Will galloped off with the posse, all riding as quickly as they had come. The rooster stretched out his neck and flapped his wings and scolded them mightily.

A few hours of steady riding brought them to Mankato. Trotting down into the valley, the sheriff said, "We'll stop at the Rock Street Livery to rest and water the horses."

From there they walked down Front Street to the Clifton House Hotel, the unofficial Mankato headquarters around which hundreds of people had gathered. Tense, excited voices filled the air.

Stopping a ways back from the crowd, Sheriff Barton said, "Lots of uniforms here. There's a couple of sheriffs, and over there's some military, some police officers from St. Paul." He pointed to the hotel entrance.

"Ara!" called a deep voice. "Ara Barton." A tall lanky man wearing a Blue Earth County deputy badge strode up to Sheriff Barton and shook his hand. "Glad you could join us."

"What's been going on?" asked the sheriff.

"Early yesterday morning, the outlaws slipped

through here over the trestle bridge," said the deputy. "They captured a citizen."

"Did they hurt him?" Will blurted out. "Did he escape?"

The deputy shook his head. "The man claims they let him go. They had questioned him pretty thorough about roads and routes that might be left unguarded." The deputy spit on the ground. "I guess the outlaws thought he was too scared to talk. They made him swear to keep his mouth shut and then let him go free."

Henry leaned close to Will and whispered, "Those outlaws will be mighty mad when they realize their hostage reported it straightaway. They won't be so generous next time."

"Sheriff Dill is still out where the man said he'd been held, trying to pick up a trail. He sent me back to report," said the deputy.

Before Sheriff Barton could reply, they heard a raspy voice yell, "Sheriff! Sheriff!"

Turning, they all saw a red-faced young man sprinting toward them with, shirttails loose and flapping. He waved his arms, too out of breath to call again. He stopped dead in his tracks in front of Sheriff Barton and leaned over, hands on his knees. He drew in deep gasping lungfuls of air.

"This here's Richard Roberts," said the deputy. "Lives out near Lake Crystal."

Sheriff Barton put a hand on the young man's back and stood him upright. "What'd you see, boy?" he asked.

"Two outlaws broke through . . . ," Richard gasped, "our pickets at Lake Crystal." He gulped in another breath. "Whipping their horses. Rode like the—*gasp*—devil hisself was chasing 'em." He put his hand to his chest and drew in a slow steady breath of air. "We shot at them. I think I might have wounded one of them in the leg," he said, his breathing having returned somewhat to normal.

Startled by this turn of events, the deputy yelled, "I'll tell General Pope!" He ran toward the hotel as if he'd been shot out of a cannon.

"That means they're still nearby! Let's ride!" said Sheriff Barton, running back to the stable. Will chased right behind him, Henry and Manning close on their heels.

"Wait for me!" shouted Richard. "I'll show you where they were heading."

"They won't get away from us again!" Will yelled.

DESPERATE
AND DANGEROUS
Sunday, September 17, 1876

Hoarfrost sparkled on the overhanging branches as the rising sun glinted off the trees surrounding the posse's campsite. Will, cold and stiff from sleeping on the hard ground, gathered his gear together. They'd ridden steadily westward for four days, resting only long enough to spare the horses. Their hard pursuit had never brought them within sight of the outlaws. Good thing Richard Roberts came along. He was a good tracker. They'd have lost that trail long ago without his help.

Will shared half of his last apple with Buck as he saddled him. He hoped whoever was riding Star was taking good care of her. Still munching, Buck pawed the frosty ground, eager to move out. Will tightened the cinch and threw on the saddlebags.

"These two can't be hurt too badly," Henry had surmised. "Nothing seems to slow them down. They must have split the gang up and left the wounded ones behind."

"That would mean they're getting desperate," said Will.

"And more dangerous," agreed Henry.

They kept up a steady canter, pushing their horses to their limits. Will appreciated Buck's strength and stamina. He wished Pa could see that horses other than draft horses had those qualities.

Richard, in the lead, called a halt. He got off his horse and walked through the prairie grass, moving the long blades apart, studying the ground. He straightened up and scanned the far distance.

"They seem to be headed toward that ranch yonder," he said, shading his eyes with his hand. "Maybe they stopped for food or fresh horses."

A steady hour's canter brought them into a neat farmstead surrounded by a grove of cedar trees and trimmed lilac hedges. A neat and tidy farmwife stepped out of the house to greet them. A big gray cat twined itself around her ankles.

"Good morning, gentlemen," she said.

Sheriff Barton took off his hat. "Morning, ma'am. Could you tell us, ma'am, have you seen two men, perhaps injured, go by this way?"

The farmwife was nodding her head before the sheriff finished his question. "Most certainly have. Would they be the Northfield bank robbers?"

"We think so, ma'am," the sheriff answered.

Not stopping for breath between her words, the woman spoke quickly. "Land sakes, I gave them breakfast. They were full of questions about telegraphs and railroads. Made me downright suspicious. As soon as they left, I sent my husband to inform our county sheriff. They're probably out hunting them too by now." She pointed across the prairie. "The robbers rode west. Probably headed for Sioux Falls or Yankton."

"Thank you kindly, ma'am," said the sheriff, turning back to the main road.

Will held Buck back long enough to ask, "Did you notice what kind of horses they rode?"

The farmwife shrugged. "Dark, I guess. Tired."

Will's voice trembled a bit as he asked, "Could one have been a mare? A pretty chestnut mare with a white star on her forehead?"

She shook her head slightly. "I didn't take notice. Sorry."

After another hour's ride, the posse stopped at a creek for water, resting the horses. They ate biscuits and jerky from their rations, washed it down with creek water. They couldn't afford to waste time. The outlaws sure wouldn't stop to cook.

Riding steadily again, Will took note of how the landscape changed the farther west they rode. The lakes and forests of central Minnesota gave way to low rolling hills and vast prairies, the big sky stretching above it all. He couldn't help but take pleasure in riding the strong stallion across the grassy plains. Topping a high rise, the posse stopped for a moment to scan the distance ahead of them.

"There!" shouted Will. "There they are, headed down that draw!" He stood up in his stirrups, pointing into the mid-afternoon sun.

As he spoke, two faraway horsemen vanished behind a low hill.

"Let's go get 'em," called the sheriff, spurring his horse to a gallop.

The tired horses sensed the urgency. Will didn't have to encourage Buck. He quickly took the lead.

The terrain changed. The low hills became higher, the valleys deeper. Will got fleeting glimpses of the riders between hills, then they disappeared again.

"Faster, Buck," he urged, not realizing he was outdistancing the rest of the posse. The rifle slung over his shoulder slapped constantly against Will's back, forcing him to think of what he might have to do.

Cresting a steep ridge at top speed, Will thought he heard the crack of a rifle, and he imagined a bullet whizzed past him. He looked wildly in all directions at the valley below him, a jumble of ravines, boulders, and sharp rocky outcrops.

"Take cover!" yelled the sheriff from behind him. "They're holing up! They intend to make a stand." Bullets pinged and zinged and ricocheted around them as they dashed into a dry creek bed. The horses stumbled over loose stones and rotted driftwood.

Will jumped off Buck, taking his rifle in his hand. He climbed to the top of the ridge, lay flat on his stomach, and peered over the flat stone outcrop.

Henry crawled up beside him. "Think they spotted us here?" he asked, and just then a bullet splintered a small sapling next to him. They both ducked down and scrambled a few feet back down the draw. This time they came up behind brush and dried grasses. Will carefully brought up his rifle, poking the barrel through scruffy tumbleweed.

"Can't see anything but brush," complained Will. His breathing gradually slowed, but his heart kept up a steady thumping. Bullets steadily pinged near them, though not as close as before. "I can't even see where their shots are coming from."

"Do you think you can use that?" Henry asked him, nodding at the rifle Will gripped tightly. "Could you shoot a man? If one of those outlaws were in your sights, would you fire?"

"Sure I would," Will said. He looked into Henry's searching eyes. "I'm pretty sure I would. They're killers. They killed innocent people in Northfield. They're trying to kill us!" His voice gained strength. A bullet hit a boulder just above and to his left, sending stone fragments flying. "These outlaws are fleeing justice. They won't surrender. They'll go on to kill more people. They have to be stopped." Will was talking fast, nodding his head for emphasis. "You killed an outlaw in Northfield."

"Didn't have much choice," replied Henry. "It was kill or be killed. But if that's Frank or Jesse down there, and you had them in your sights, would you shoot?"

Will squirmed a bit, fingering the trigger, looking back out through the brush.

"I would fire," he said, speaking slower now, "but I would try to wound them, not kill them. Shoot at their legs or something like that." He breathed a sigh, like he had made a big decision. "I wouldn't let them escape. I would stop them."

Bullets ripped through the small covering bush that hid them and sprayed the entire outcrop the posse hid behind. Everyone crouched farther down behind the rocks. After a few moments of concentrated fire from the outlaws, it became quiet again.

"Now what?" asked Will.

"Follow me," said the sheriff. "We'll find a better position farther on." They crawled slowly down the ravine, looking for a place where they would be covered and still be able to see the outlaws. Hastily they settled themselves behind stumps and boulders. No one could see any sign of the outlaws. They waited and watched for several minutes, not wanting to reveal their new position.

Richard shouted, "They're gone! They must have moved out while we came down this ravine."

Sheriff Barton quickly climbed to the top of the

ridge and held his hat above the rocks. It drew no fire.

"You're right!" he called and stumbled back down the rocky scree. Everyone jumped up and ran to the horses, scrambling over loose stones and tree roots and tangled brush.

Back at the creek bed, they remounted their horses. Richard pointed due west. "They'll be heading for the Palisades. It's a huge rocky outcrop along the Big Sioux River. They'll lose us there for sure."

"Not if we catch them before they get there," said Barton. "We'll divide up. Henry, you and Will follow their tracks. Manning, Richard, and I will try to head them off at the river. They'll have to find a ford to cross. The Big Sioux is a rough river." They could see west easier now—the sun was nearing the horizon. "Not much daylight left," the sheriff warned.

Will and Henry cantered off together, their horses fresher after the brief rest. It was easy to follow the outlaw's trail through trampled prairie grass, and when they'd lose sight of it over rocky areas, they'd scout the edges till they found flattened grass again. Will didn't talk much. His stomach was in tight knots. He wanted to find the outlaws, yet, at the same time, he didn't want to.

But the outlaws needed to be stopped—the killing and robbing needed to end. And he was here, and he was part of the posse. Like Pa said, he had a duty.

Near the Big Sioux River, the rocky ridges and steep outcrops of the Palisades obscured all tracks and trails. Granite bluffs and cliffs hemmed in a churning river. The roar of white water rapids blocked out all other sounds. Evening darkened the eerie landscape. Henry and Will slowed their horses to a walk, picking their way over loose and jagged stones. They followed a winding animal trail, aware that every ridge could hide an ambush. Will felt the danger, breathed it.

He gripped his rifle with both hands, giving Buck his head. The strong stallion was surefooted, cautious, and steady, constantly flicking his ears. Will trusted Buck to alert him if they neared the outlaws. The shadows deepened at each turn. Night closed in.

"We'll lose them in the dark," whispered Henry. "They could be anywhere. Around the next corner or a mile away."

The trail branched out in two directions. One path traced the top of the bluffs. The other path dropped down to the river. Henry reined to a stop.

Shoulders slumped, he said, "It's no use trying to track them any farther. It's too dark, too rocky. Too late."

Will strained his eyes, still trying to see ahead. The darkness was so deep he couldn't tell ridge from sky. He dismounted and dropped Buck's reins. "Sheriff Barton will be along soon. I'm going to check out this river path. I'll be right back."

The sound of the rushing rapids covered any protest Henry might have made as Will slid his feet cautiously ahead, one hand on the cold, wet wall of rock. Something in the back of Will's mind told him it was too dark, that out here darkness meant danger. But he pushed it away as if it were more rain in his face—he was too close to give up. He couldn't see a thing, but the path was definitely going down. Icy spray from the rapids struck his face and hands and feet. The cold night air wrapped around Will, and he shivered. He clamped his jaw to keep his teeth from chattering.

Loose stones spread away from under his boots, and he slid down several feet, his numb hands grasping for a hold on the rock wall. Grabbing a crevice between boulders, he stopped his fall and stood upright on a slippery but level stone. He let loose of the crevice to wipe the dripping icy water off his face.

From behind him, a large hand with a grip of iron encased his arm. A steely hand clamped over his mouth.

A LIFE OF ADVENTURE
Night, September 17, 1876

Choking and gagging, Will reached up to grab the arms that pushed him into a gaping black crevice, but he couldn't budge their iron grip. Stumbling and staggering, furious at himself and at his captor, he struggled to keep his feet under him.

Forcibly propelled deep into the crevice, far from Henry, Will began to see, to make out his surroundings. Firelight reflected dimly off the granite walls looming up and over him. A small crackling campfire revealed he was in a small cavern. It narrowed into another crevice a few yards on, which Will guessed led straight through to the river. Cold air washed into the cavern, which echoed with the nearby rumbling roar of rapids.

The strong arms dragged him close to the campfire, where another man roughly grasped

Will's wrists and bound them together in front of Will with a strip of rawhide. They forced him to sit and then tied his ankles together. His mouth was free, but he kept silent, though panting rapidly. The two men squatted in front of Will. Firelight glinted off a pistol barrel aimed at Will's chest. He steadied his breathing and looked into their faces.

He saw surprise in both of them.

"It's the Sasse kid!" said Frank. "Are you with the posse that's been hounding us?" He pulled back the hammer on the Colt revolver. It made a very loud click.

"Hold on, Frank," said Jesse. "You ain't going to shoot anyone. These Yankee posses would be on us quicker than a duck on a june bug."

Relief shuddered through Will as Frank holstered the pistol.

"Keep quiet, now," warned Frank. "You yell, you die. Hey, have you still got Raider? How is he? Was he hurt bad?"

Will had to swallow a couple of times before he could get words out of his mouth. "Raider?" he asked. "The buckskin stallion? He's fine now. Wasn't hurt too bad."

Frank leaned closer to Will. "Is he with you now? Have you been riding him?"

"Yes, but . . . , " Will started to say.

"We can't get Raider now, Frank!" interrupted Jesse. "The kid left him on top of the bluff with the rest of the posse. Besides, we can't bring him."

Frank shrugged, walked over to the fire, and threw on a few small branches. Will sat up as straight as he could with his legs bound together.

"Where's my mare?" he asked. "Are you still riding her?"

Jesse smiled at Will. "Don't worry about her, we didn't ride her into the ground. She's too nice a mare to ruin her. Don't recollect where we left her, though. Do you, Frank?" He looked over at Frank, who just dragged over a couple of large driftwood logs, laying them alongside the fire. He lashed the ends together with a well-worn rope. Jesse went to help him. The two worked fast, sure of what they were doing.

"Where are your horses? Why are you building a raft?" asked Will.

Frank came back and sat on his heels in front of Will, grinning. His teeth gleamed in the firelight.

"Didn't you see the jump? You weren't with the posse that was chasing us?" He stood up and gestured with his arms how they had escaped. "We had come to this narrow gorge. I think it was called

Devil's Gulch. Right, Jesse?"

Jesse kept working. "Sounds like it," he said.

Frank stood over Will. A burning branch snapped and sparks flared up, making Frank's face a leering mask. "We slipped off the horses at the last minute, gave them a whack with a rawhide strip, and they jumped the gorge. It was nearly dark. The posse saw the horses jump and thought we were still on them." He laughed. "They didn't care to make the jump themselves. Probably figure we're well into Dakota Territory by now."

"Frank," called Jesse. "Come over here and finish this raft. We might not have much time." Chuckling to himself, Frank went back to lashing logs together.

"Why did you come to Minnesota?" Will asked. "And why did you pick the Northfield bank to rob?"

"We came here because of Ames Mill," said Jesse.

"Ames Mill?" asked Will, puzzled. "Why?"

"Adelbert Ames got himself elected Mississippi governor," said Jesse. "He and his father-in-law, General Butler, gave us Southerners a rough time after the Civil War. We thought we'd return the favor."

"We did that, all right!" laughed Frank. "We sure shot up his town. Folks won't soon forget the day the James boys came to Northfield!" Still laughing, he and Jesse dragged the raft to the cavern entrance facing the river. Will watched in silence.

Jesse came over to Will as Frank maneuvered the raft to the rocky riverbank. He sat next to Will and he leaned on a boulder slightly warmed by the fire. "How about Cole and the boys?" Jesse asked. "Were they caught?"

"No," said Will. "No one knows where Cole is, or the others with him. But Clell is dead. So's another man. Someone thought he recognized him. Said he was called Bill Stiles."

Jesse looked away, shaking his head. "We rode together with Quantrell's Rangers in the war. No Yankee ever caught us then. And no Yankee ever will catch us alive." He stood and turned to Frank. "Can that raft make it across the river? The posse will be out looking for Will, here. Let's get ourselves into Dakota."

"Ready to go," said Frank. "Going to leave the kid here?"

The firelight caught Jesse's dark eyes, lit with excitement. "What do you say, Will? Want to join us? Live a life of adventure?" He took out a bowie knife, ready to cut the rawhide off Will's wrists. "You sure don't want to spend the rest of your life on that little eighty acres, clomping along behind a clumsy workhorse pulling a plough. Come with us. It seems we need another gang member."

Jesse grinned at Will, his eyes and teeth gleaming in the reflected firelight. "You'll have the best horses. You can have anything you want. It's all yours for the taking. Ride with us."

Will looked up at Jesse, a tall black figure silhouetted by the flickering embers. Shadows danced on the dark rugged rock behind him.

Will's glance dropped to Jesse's waist, to Jesse's hands on his holstered guns. The campfire snapped and crackled, a flare of sparks flashed in the dark. The gleaming steel hammer of the revolver on Jesse's right twinkled in the sudden light, seeming to wink at Will. To beckon him.

Staring at the gun, Will said as though talking to it, "My pa bought me a nice rifle the day of the bank robbery for hunting game. Now I've found out I'd use it to stop an outlaw. There's power in a gun. Over life and death. Power to get whatever you want and to get rid of what you don't want. He looked back up into Jesse's eyes. "I guess what

I want most is law and order. Security for my family. A safe home and good living." A rueful smile played around his mouth. "Guess I have what I want."

Jesse stood silent for a minute, then put the knife back in its sheath. "I'm glad we crossed paths, Will Sasse. Thank your lucky stars you never had to go to war. You'd be a different person." He turned and was gone.

There was no sound other than the rushing water. Light faded as the flames died down and darkness crept close around Will. He shivered. Cold seeped into his legs and back. Slumping back against the rock, Will drew his knees up in front of him. The relief that he wasn't to blame for the robbery by inviting the James brothers to his farm faded away and disappeared, a small pebble dropped into a very deep well. His head dropped between his bound arms and rested on his knees.

"Will? Are you in there? Are you all right?" Henry's worried voice echoed through the black cavern.

A feeling of failure settled into Will's bones along with the cold, damp stiffness.

HOME AGAIN
Night, September 20, 1876

A crescent moon dimly lit Will's path as he cantered home. It was late, but a lantern shone in the
house, silhouetting Ma in the kitchen. Will could
see Pa get up from the porch rocker and stride
toward Will as he reined up by the barn door. The
barn doors creaked open and Buck eagerly entered
a stall. Will started to unsaddle him.

Pa followed Will inside the barn, scowling.
"Where in tarnation have you been? It's been over
a week! Does it take that long to chase down a
couple of wounded outlaws?" His voice was rough
and loud, impatient.

Will slid the saddle off Buck's back and threw it
onto the stall sideboards, then turned to loosen the
bridle. "We followed them all the way to the
Dakota border, Pa, riding hard all the way." He

hung the bridle on its peg beside the stall. Returning Pa's look, anger rising in his own voice, Will said, "And we lost them there, late at night. It was Frank and Jesse, and they got across a rocky river gorge into Dakota Territory. I don't suppose anyone can track them now." He turned back to put a halter on Buck, then began brushing him down.

Pa shook his head in disgust. "Waste of valuable time," he said. "I don't suppose you got anywhere near them."

Will kept his back turned, brushing Buck vigorously. "Oh, I got close enough. I was scouting alone one night. I stumbled right into their hideout."

Pa grabbed Will's shoulder, turning Will to look directly into his face. "You did what? What'd they do? What'd they say?" he said harshly.

Anger flooded Will as he glared at Pa. Turning his back again, he tersely told Pa what had happened in the cavern, and why the James gang had come to Northfield.

Disgusted, Pa said, "Shot up our town to settle a grudge? How did killing and robbing innocent people ever settle anything?" Pa again grabbed Will's shoulder, roughly turning him. "Did they threaten to hurt you?"

Will pulled away. "Frank held a gun on me, till he saw who I was. But they didn't hurt me." Will's words were short, clipped, and angry. "Jesse even asked if I wanted to join their gang."

"Good grief, son!" Pa all but shouted, banging his fist against the wall. Buck jumped back, snorting and rearing. "Don't you ever stop to think of what you're doing? How could you not realize the danger you were walking into?" Pa walked out of the stall, slamming the half-door.

Will held onto Buck's halter, calming him. Anger seethed through Will. He would have shouted back at Pa, but he had his hands full with the buckskin stallion.

Pa stopped again. His knuckles were white as he gripped the stall door. "At first light tomorrow, I want you out harvesting corn."

"Wait, Pa!" called Will, still holding Buck. "The Younger brothers might still be around here. If the posse has to ride again, they'll come by for me." Will held his breath.

Pa turned and glared at Will, his jaws clamped tight. Will stared right back.

"It's still my duty," he reminded Pa.

Pa stared a moment more, then said, "If the posse has a chance to trail the Youngers, we'll both ride. I'll get Jeb Anderson's saddle horse." There was absolute finality in Pa's voice. "If I let you go alone, you'd most likely get yourself killed."

He turned and stomped away. The barn door slammed hard.

Will turned back to Buck, putting his face against the horse's heavy mane. The stallion stood quiet, as if it were now his turn to calm the boy's distress. Will didn't try to stop the sobs. He put his arm over Buck's neck, leaning into him.

Maybe he should take Buck and ride away. He could make it on his own. Get a job on some farm or in a livery stable. Gradually the shuddering sobs slowed, and Will stepped back and finished brushing Buck.

Will gave Pete and Penny a quick brushing, too. He was in no hurry to go into the house. Pete nudged him gently, glad to see him. Penny rubbed her face against his arm. Molly and Mae, in the next stall, nickered at him too, wanting their share of attention.

Last he went to his little filly. She was curled up in the hay, long spindly legs tucked under her. She lifted her head and looked at him, head cocked and ears flicked forward. She looked so little, so lonely without Star. He walked away before she got up.

It would be awfully hard to leave them all.

He blew out the lantern and walked slowly to the house. Ma had left a light in the window. As he went inside, Ma rose from her rocking chair, laying her knitting aside. She came to him and put her arms around him.

"We were so scared for you, son," she whispered. "It's good to have you home." Will hugged her back.

CRUSHED MINT
Thursday, September 21, 1876

"We should get there pretty soon," shouted Henry, riding at a brisk canter alongside Will. They followed just behind Sheriff Barton, Manning, and Pa. The morning was murky, the road mucky. Hooves threw up clods of mud. Henry continued, "The telegraph from Madelia reported four outlaws spotted crossing the bridge near the lakes. Watowan County sheriff's in pursuit."

Will said nothing, riding with shoulders hunched forward.

"It has to be the Younger brothers," Henry said. "It's been two weeks since the raid. I reckon they've been hiding out all this while."

"Reckon so," Will finally said, glaring ahead at Pa's back. Sheriff Barton had made no comment when Pa announced he was riding with them. The sheriff hadn't even seem surprised, as if Will couldn't take care of himself. Pa rode right beside the sheriff, like he'd been riding with the posse all along.

The packed dirt road curved around a wide lake, gray now with rain clouds reflecting off its rain-dappled surface. Autumn leaves that were still on the trees dripped and drooped. A dim popping sounded up ahead.

"Gunshots!" called Sheriff Barton. He pulled his hat down firmly, leaned forward and urged his horse to a gallop. The others stayed close behind him.

They clattered across the wood slats of the Watowan River Bridge. Rain clouds obscured a limestone bluff ahead of them. The road sand-wiched itself between the bluffs and river bottom woods: willows, box elders, and wild plum trees. Spreading grapevines tangled it all together. Will felt cool, misty air lick his face.

Rounding a curve, the road widened and left the riverside. Wooded hills and brushy thickets hemmed the ditches. Several men stood in the road ahead of them. A patrol of armed men, some on foot and some on horseback, blocked the width of the road. They had weapons drawn and ready.

Steady gunfire and frenzied shouts encased the thicket they guarded. None of the men looked eager to go in there.

Sheriff Barton reined up beside a guard holding the reins of several horses, all shying from the noise and bumping each other and snorting.

"What's the situation?" the sheriff demanded.

"Sheriff Glispin went in with six men to bring the bandits out, dead or alive," the guard said, pulling the reins of horses, now neighing and rearing and kicking at each other.

"We're going in," said Sheriff Barton. The posse dismounted and quickly tied their horses to the branches of a downed tree. The sheriff led them in, following a trail of broken branches and torn grapevines. Gun smoke, acrid and angry, hung in the misty air. As Will crept through the tangled overgrowth, his shirt snagged on raspberry thorns and burrs stuck to his pants. The trampled path disappeared. Will saw nothing ahead but bushes and vines and prickly ash.

"Sheriff Glispin won't know we've come into the woods," Will whispered to Henry. "His posse will shoot at us. They'll mistake us for the outlaws."

"Stay low," said Henry. "Don't draw attention

to yourself. Don't fire unless you're absolutely sure who is in your sights."

Sheriff Barton motioned his men to fan out. Pa went left, next to the sheriff. Will angled right away from them, following Henry.

They climbed a slight rise. Peering down through a stand of sumac, Will saw Sheriff Glispin's posse hunkered down, exchanging rifle fire with the outlaws in the thicket just beyond them.

"How can they see anyone in there? It's solid brush," said Will. He watched a posse member rise up on one knee and fire into the bushes. The dull thunk of a bullet hitting something solid followed the crack of the man's rifle.

"They can see something. Return fire is coming from one or two places," said Henry. He crouched and stepped around a thorny raspberry patch. Will followed him, still watching the posse.

A raspberry cane whipped back as Henry, just ahead of Will, passed under it. It hit Will in the face with a sharp snap. He yelped, jumped back, and reached for his cheek. Suddenly someone thudded into him and knocked him flat. He landed with his face in wet moldy leaves, the weight of a body pinning him. Will struggled up to his hands and knees and the body rolled off. He heard a low moan.

Henry knelt beside him. "Keep down," he whispered. "We're under fire."

Will wiped mud and moss and wet leaves off his face. Turning, he saw Pa lying on his side, his back to Will. Blood seeped out of his shoulder, spreading as his shirt absorbed it. He hadn't made a sound after the first moan.

"Pa!" gasped Will. Henry was ripping Pa's bloody shirt apart.

"How bad is it? It's not real bad, is it?" Will's hoarse voice whispered.

Pa didn't answer. He lay with his eyes shut and jaws clenched.

Henry exposed the wound and inspected it front and back. The bullet had entered Pa's chest close to his left shoulder. Henry's fingers probed. Pa gritted his teeth.

"Pa, are you all right?" Will asked, wishing he'd been shot instead of Pa. He hadn't been quiet. He could have gotten everyone killed.

Pa's head hung low, his face almost in the leaves. Will snatched off his jacket, rolled it into a ball, and eased it under Pa's head. Gunfire and yelling continued like nothing had happened. No one else noticed that Pa was shot, that he lay bleeding.

Henry pulled off his own shirt and ripped it into strips. "Use your shirt, too, Will. Tear it like this." Henry folded a couple of strips into bandages and put them over the bullet wounds, front and back. "It's not too bad, Mr. Sasse. The bullet went right through, just like Alonzo Bunker's." He used the pieces of Will's shirt to hold the bandages in place.

The shooting below them sounded farther from the thicket, as Sheriff Glispin's posse closed in on the outlaws. Will rose up on his knees but couldn't see anything. He turned back to Pa. Even in the cold air, sweat ran down Pa's face. Will patted it off with a strip of his shirt. Henry reached across Pa and wiped a smear of blood off Will's face.

"That branch gave you a nasty cut, Will," Henry said. "I'm sorry. I should have been more careful."

Will nodded, eyes on Pa. He wished Pa would say something, not just lie there.

Henry and Will helped Pa up into a sitting position, leaning him against a big cottonwood tree. The tangy smell of crushed mint leaves rose from the damp ground where Pa had lain. Henry and Will sat beside Pa. Dew fell off the overhanging branches and splattered on Will's bare back and he shivered. Pa had gone awfully pale.

"How'd you know I'd be shot at, Pa? How'd you know to jump in front of me?" Will asked.

Henry wrapped his coat around Pa and reached for Will's deerskin jacket. He shook it out and spread it over Pa's chest.

Pa exhaled a deep shuddering breath. "I just happened to glance toward the thicket," he whispered. "I saw the glint of a gun barrel, drawing a bead on someone. When I heard that yelp, I knew the gun was aimed at you." Pa's whole body shivered. "Thank God I was close enough. And fast enough."

"I'm sorry, Pa," said Will. "I should have kept my mouth shut." Will knew this was all his fault. It should be him, not Pa, that got shot.

"Cease fire!" Sheriff Glispin hollered from the thicket below, his voice carrying over the sound of gunfire through the surrounding woods, echoing off the limestone bluffs.

Henry looked away. "Did they surrender?" he asked.

Pa managed a weak smile at Will. "Wasn't your fault," he said. "I saw that gun barrel draw a bead before you yelped. And I'd have pushed anyone aside. You'd have done the same."

"Hold your fire!" Sheriff Glispin yelled to his men. To the outlaws in the thicket he ordered, "Lay down your guns and come out!"

Will raised up on his knees and looked down the slope. Sheriff Glispin's posse moved in closer. Slowly, step by step, they advanced. It grew deathly quiet. A breeze blew cold mist past Will, and he shivered again.

Everyone watched silently, motionless and listening.

A sharp gust of wind rattled the branches, shaking water off the wet leaves. It carried an answer back from the depths of the thicket.

"I surrender. They are all down but me!"

Brush and brambles snapped and cracked as Glispen and his men entered the thicket. From far away cracked the shot of a distant rifle.

"I said, hold your fire!" Sheriff Glispin's angry words reverberated through the woods and echoed off the limestone bluff where the shot had come from.

Will stood up alongside the cottonwood, trying to see who had shot after the cease-fire order. Glispin and his men had disappeared into the woods. Henry darted past Will, scrambling down a sandy bank, avoiding exposed tree roots.

"That's Bob Younger!" Will heard Sheriff Glispin shout. Henry was also calling instructions. *Good*, thought Will. The outlaws were only wounded. Not killed.

Will went back to Pa, who looked better—not so white, breathing easier. "Think you can get up, Pa? I can help you up. You can sit in one of the wagons back on the road."

"Can't stay here all day," said Pa. He put his good arm over Will's shoulder and leaned forward. Will got his arms behind and around Pa. Bracing himself, he pulled Pa to his feet. Slowly they made their way back. Will could hear the others coming behind them. No one worried about being quiet anymore.

Will reached open roadway. "Lend a hand here!" he called. A couple of guards lifted Pa and carried him to a buckboard and hoisted him up to the wagon seat.

"Tarnation!" Pa spluttered. "I can walk just fine! You don't see a bullet hole in my leg, do you?"

Will had to grin.

The rest of the posses struggled out of the thorny woods, carrying four men over to the buckboard. Will quickly lowered the gate. They heaved in a body, all shot up and bloody.

"This one's dead," someone said. Will climbed up into the wagon box and positioned the body against a sideboard. He looked carefully at the face. Not one he knew.

None too gently, posse members hoisted the other three outlaws, all bleeding from several bullet wounds each, into the wagon box. Henry jumped up beside Will and they helped lay the outlaws down.

"Move out!" called Henry. "We've got to get these men back to town." The gate slammed shut. The extra horses, including the outlaws', were tied to the back of the wagon. Star was not there. The younger brothers hadn't had her, either.

"Here," said Henry, handing more shirt strips to Will. "Stop their bleeding."

Will sat back. There was so much blood on their faces, Will couldn't tell who they were. He knelt beside the closest man, trying to wipe blood off his face. He'd been shot in the jaw, but Will recognized him after all.

"Rest easy, Cole," he whispered, wrapping a bandage around his head. Cole's chin bled heavily. He looked up at Will with a flicker of gratitude, then closed his eyes.

"Henry," said Will, "Pa doesn't seem to be hurt

too bad. Will his arm be all right? Will he be able to use it? To work again?"

"Most likely," answered Henry. "I'll know better when I can clean the wound out and see how much damage the bullet did."

As the two posses and the wagons neared Madelia, crowds of people ran to meet them, cheering and waving as if it were a Fourth of July parade. "News sure spreads fast," remarked Henry. "Good thing, too. Glispin's posse deserves a hero's welcome."

"Take them into my hotel," said Colonel Vought, one of Sheriff Glispin's men. "They need medical attention and food before you can jail them." The wagons pulled up in front of a white frame building with a wide veranda across the front. The excited crowd gathered around as the injured outlaws were helped into the Flanders House Inn.

Cole managed to tip his hat to them, a crooked grin on his bandaged face. The crowd cheered.

Will and Henry stood back as the onlookers flocked closer. "Seems even the outlaws are glad this ordeal is over," said Henry.

"It won't be over for me till I get Star back," said Will.

STRAIGHT ANSWERS
Friday, September 22, 1876

The next morning, while Pa was downstairs having breakfast, Will walked quietly down the hotel's long hallway to the door of Cole's room. He knocked, heard a noise, and went in. Cole looked much better washed, bandaged, and wearing clean clothes. He was sitting up in bed, eating a bowl of hot oatmeal to which someone had generously added brown sugar.

Cole greeted Will with a warm smile. "Almost as good as your Ma's cooking." His wounded chin didn't seem to hinder either his eating or his talking.

"Reckon so," Will agreed. He pulled a straight chair alongside Cole's bed.

Cole's smiled faded. "What happened to the others?" he asked. "Did you hear?"

Will knew Cole was referring to Frank and Jesse. He looked down at his hands, tightly gripping his hat brim. "Reckon they crossed the Big Sioux River at the Palisades and escaped into Dakota Territory."

Cole laughed. "Reckon not!"

Will looked up quickly. "Jesse told me that's where they were headed."

"You talked to them?" asked Cole, grinning at Will.

Will felt his cheeks get hot and looked down at his hat again. "Yeah," he admitted. "They sorta captured me. They were building a raft to cross the river." He looked up at Cole, who was still grinning.

"They didn't go across the river," Cole said and laughed again. "The plan was to steal a boat and ride down the Big Sioux River till it joined the Missouri River, and ride that all the way back to Missouri."

Will's hat brim was nearly crushed. He leaned back against the hard knobby rungs of his chair. It felt like the hard, rough rock he had leaned against in the river canyon. Looking out the window, Will didn't see the bright morning sun. He saw flickering shadows and heard rushing river rapids.

"Jesse told me you came to Northfield to get even with Mr. Ames," he said, his voice raising at the end to make it a question.

Cole ate the toasted bread from his tray, savoring every bite. "That's so. Yankee governor!" he said, scorn dripping from his voice like the butter off his toast. "We had a score to settle with him and his father-in-law, General Butler." He licked a little stream of butter running down his fingers and added, "Look in my coat pocket. For a newspaper clipping."

Will hung his battered hat on the bedpost and walked over to the clothes cupboard. He reached in the deep pockets of Cole's ragged, dirty duster, avoiding the bloodstains. He brought out a folded piece of newsprint.

Sitting on the edge of his chair, Will opened it carefully. It was from the *Rice County Journal*, dated a month before the bank raid.

> The First National Bank of this place is having a new set of doors put into their vault. Two doors will have to be opened before the vault is reached. . . . A steel burglar-proof safe will avoid the annoyance of having burglars pull the cashier's hair to make him open the safe as it cannot be opened by anyone until a certain hour. . . .

Will looked slowly up at Cole, who was still engrossed in his meal. "That's why you were here so long. You were planning everything ahead."

Cole swallowed a long drink of coffee.

"We always do," he said. "Besides evening the score with Ames and Butler, we figured a bank that needed such a fancy vault would have a lot of money in it. We'd heard Ames and Butler alone had deposited seventy-five thousand dollars."

With a wistful look at his now-empty cup, Cole said, "I guess we should have found out the hour the safe could be opened. We missed out on a lot of money."

Will shook his head. "Wouldn't have done you any good," he said. "The safe wasn't locked. Just closed. And there wasn't more than fifteen thousand dollars in it." He smiled ruefully. "Including fifty dollars that my pa had just deposited."

Cole put his hand over his eyes, slowly rubbing his forehead, muttering under his breath. Will caught the words, "liquored up" and "darn fools." He looked up at Will.

"The sheriff asked me last night who had killed the cashier, Heywood," he said. "I told him I'd give him an answer this morning. Can you get me a pen and paper?"

Will rummaged through a small desk against the hotel room wall. He found a scrap of paper and a blunt quill pen. In the back of the drawer was a bottle of ink. It was good enough for Cole. He quickly scratched out a message, folded the paper, and gave it to Will. "Hand this to the sheriff on your way out, Will."

Will turned it over in his hands, wondering what it said. Noticing his interest, Cole said, "You can read it."

Somewhat apprehensive, remembering watching the outlaws leave the bank, Will glanced over at Cole.

"Go ahead," Cole urged.

Opening it, Will read the strong script. *Be true to your friends till the heavens fall.* Will felt strange relief. He refolded it and put it in his shirt pocket.

"I'll give it to Sheriff Barton."

Cole returned to his oatmeal. Will bit his lip, afraid to ask. Then, in a husky voice, he said. "Where's Star?"

Cole looked up, startled. "Your mare? You haven't found her?" Looking past Will, he concentrated, obviously trying to remember. "The day after Jesse traded Raider for your mare, we left her with a farmer at a remote place near Elysian. He boarded our team and wagon. He probably still has them, and your mare."

Will took a slow deep breath. He might still find Star.

"I remember Jesse remarked he hoped the farmer had as much horse sense as your Pa," Cole added. "Hope you can get her back."

Will grabbed his rumpled hat off the bedpost.

"I'll find her!" he promised, and he bolted out the door.

REUNION
Saturday, September 23, 1876

A bright morning sun shone down on Will's back, warming bones that had been chilled for more than two weeks. Birds chirped again, and mist and rain no longer dulled the brightly colored leaves. Will resisted the urge to slap the reins over the backs of Pete and Penny, already trotting briskly. Ma, alongside him on the wagon seat, was cheerful and chatty. The sun was shining, and Star was somewhere down the road.

Sitting next to Ma, Pa chewed on a long straw, a few wheat grains still at its end. Ma had forced him to rest the day before, and his arm was in a sling, but that didn't hinder him much.

"Lucky thing we harvested good hay and grain crops this year," Pa said. "There should be enough to feed all the extra stock we have, if the winter isn't too harsh or long."

Will waited for Pa to come to the point. Ma started to look worried.

"But have you given thought to where you'll keep your horses, Will? The box stall won't hold Buck and Star and the filly." He spit out the gnawed end of the straw and started chewing again on the fresh-bit end. "Best you do some planning, son."

"You're right, Pa," said Will. "Can't leave Buck out in the pasture all winter. I'll think on it."

Pa said nothing more, just kept chewing on that straw.

The next turn in the road brought them to Farmer Quiram's homestead. The barking hound dogs bounded up and raced around the wagon. Pete and Penny never flicked an ear. Will jumped off the wagon and was on the back stoop as Mr. Quiram came out the door.

"G'day," said the farmer. "Back again?" He called off the dogs, put his pipe in his mouth, and looked toward the wagon.

From the wagon seat, Pa nodded at him. "We're looking for a farmer around here who boards horses. He might be holding some for Missouri folks."

Farmer Quiram withdrew his pipe and blew smoke in the air. "Try Stoerings'." He pointed his pipe down a narrow one-lane dirt road. "About a mile, as the crow flies."

Trotting on down the road, they discovered it was quite a bit farther than a mile. The lane wound around steep hills and small lakes, not at all 'as the crow flies'. But eventually they came to a well-tended farmsite. Two farmers, obviously a father and son, were splitting wood. The sharp fragrance of dry kindling sweetened the air. Pigeons cooed from a nearby dovecote.

Will pulled up and jumped out of the wagon. "Good morning, sir. I'm Will Sasse, from Northfield. This here's my Ma and Pa. We came to see if you're boarding horses for some folks from Missouri."

The elder Stoering spoke. "We are," he said slowly, with a German accent.

"Are you here to get them?" asked the younger. "Been quite a spell. Been wondering if someone'd come for them."

"Well," Pa said, climbing down off the wagon, "it turns out those Missouri folks were the outlaws that robbed the Northfield bank. The horses now belong to Rice County, and you can return them to Sheriff Barton at Faribault. The county will pay your boarding fee."

Farmer Stoering didn't look too surprised. "Figured it was something like that," he said. "We kinda expected someone would come looking for them."

"Except for a mare," said Pa. "If you have her, she belongs to my son."

"Pretty chestnut mare?" asked Will. "White star on her face?"

Young Stoering smiled. "Think so. I'll take you out to the pasture." The two boys ran down a grassy lane overhung on both sides by maple and oak trees. Red and orange and yellow leaves kaleidoscoped in the breeze the boys created as they raced past.

Coming into an open meadow, Will spotted his mare among a group of grazing horses and cows. She looked lovely, hale, and healthy. "Star!" he called, vaulting the rail fence and running toward her. "Star!"

The mare raised her head and flicked her ears forward. Immediately she raced toward Will. They fairly crashed into each other. Will wrapped his arms around her neck, burying his face in her mane. "Star. Star," he repeated softly.

After a moment, Star tossed her head up, stepping back to nuzzle Will's chest. She pushed her head against him, nickering softly. Will patted her face, her neck, telling her how glad he was to have her back.

Pa and the Stoerings came up to them, grinning. "Guess that's his horse, all right," said the boy.

"No question about that," agreed Mr. Stoering.

Pa reached up and straightened Star's forelock.

"Your fancy little filly's sure going to be happy to see you!" Pa told her.

Will realized that all the while he had been gone with the posse, Pa had looked after Star's foal. And he had done all Will's chores. And had never complained about it.

As they walked back up the lane, Pa complimented the Stoerings on their fine horse stock. He talked about the team of Belgians he had bought that summer. Soon he and Farmer Stoering were debating purebred draft horses versus grade horses, both of them talking at once. Will and young Stoering followed, speaking of riding and driving horses. Star pranced beside them, tossing her head.

At the farmyard, Ma was visiting with Mrs. Stoering. The women petted and fussed over Star,

Ma reaching into her apron pocket and unwrapping a handkerchief full of sugar to feed to Star.

Mrs. Stoering insisted they stay for lunch. Pa objected briefly, mentioning he had hay in the field that needed to be put up, but Mr. Stoering persuaded him (easily, Will thought) that it would be all the better for extra drying time.

When Ma and Mrs. Stoering prepared lunch, Pa told Mr. Stoering and his boy about the bank raid and the pursuit of the outlaws.

"The James boys narrowly escaped," he said. "But the Younger brothers were captured and are awaiting trial at Faribault." He went on to tell about the shoot-out at Madelia, making light of his gunshot wound. As Pa talked about the details of the capture, Will stood beside Star, brushing his fingers through her mane.

"Listen to Pa," he said softly. "He really doesn't blame me for his getting shot. But he had been so angry at me for getting caught by Frank and Jesse."

Star nudged Will's shoulder, sniffing his pockets for an apple or a carrot. Will brushed along Star's back and down her side, pulling out pasture burrs. He guessed Pa had had a right to be angry. Being careless could certainly get a body killed. He wished he hadn't needed to learn that the hard way.

Will stopped brushing. Deftly he felt down Star's side, along her belly.

"Star! You're with foal!" He put his arms around her neck and hid his tears in her mane. After a bit, he brushed and petted her till lunch was ready, and even then hated to leave her long enough to eat.

All through the meal, Will looked out the window at Star. He heard Pa offer to pay for Star's board and the Stoerings insist she had eaten nothing but pasture grass. Finally back outside, he lifted the saddle out of the buckboard and put it on Star. She pawed the ground, eager to go home. Will vaulted up onto the saddle and Star reared playfully.

Mane and tail flying, ears pricked forward, Star galloped down the road. The afternoon sun glinted through shimmering leaves. Lights and shadows danced along the tree-lined road.

Will leaned slightly forward as he rode, one hand on Star's neck, feeling rippling muscles. Heading home to Buck and his little filly, a wild spreading joy filled his heart. He had his breeding herd now!

TIGHT QUARTERS
October 18, 1876

Will walked back home along the meadow path, breathing the bracing morning air. It smelled of freshly plowed earth and wild grapes. He passed the neat corn shocks he and Pa had stacked, laden with long ears drying in the autumn sun. Pa saw him come into the barnyard.

"How was hunting this morning? Any luck?" he called. Will grinned, holding out two pheasants.

"Ma won't have to butcher one of her chickens for Sunday dinner," he said.

Hearing approaching hoofbeats, they both turned toward the driveway. Henry Wheeler came cantering up the drive on his familiar black gelding. He dismounted and shook hands with both of them.

"Came to say good-bye before I go back to

medical college," he said. "And I wanted to ask how your injury was healing, Mr. Sasse."

"Coming along fine, according to Doc Coons," said Pa. "Danged nuisance working one-handed, but Will pretty much makes up for it." He took Will's rifle and the pheasants up to the house, leaving Will and Henry to talk.

They strolled over and sat on a willow bench Will had made for Ma near her garden. The tangy scent of Ma's mint patch made Will feel that he had a lot to make up for, not just farm work. He picked a couple of mint leaves and rubbed them between his fingers, releasing their fragrance.

"I'm glad the fall turned nice for harvesting," he said.

"It's a fall we'll never forget," said Henry. "I heard this morning the Youngers pleaded guilty and were sentenced to life in Stillwater Prison."

"That so?" asked Will. "That happened fast."

"If they'd gone to trial and were found guilty, they could have been hanged. I guess they preferred a long prison sentence to a short rope," Henry said. "Besides, there's always the possibility of parole."

Will looked out over the garden rows at ripening pumpkins. "I bet they wished they'd never heard of Minnesota," said Will. "Their bank raid was a total failure. They got no money from the bank, three of their gang were killed, and most of the rest of them got shot up pretty bad."

"Not to mention losing all their valuable horses and equipment," added Henry.

Will remembered Cole's noble message, *Be true to your friends till the heavens fall.*

It didn't seem noble when he thought of Mr. Heywood, the Swedish farmer Mr. Gustafson, and Mr. Bunker. And Pa. Cole's message—his loyalty—wasn't noble at all when weighed against the crime it covered. Will stood up. "Come over to the corral. I'll show you Star." They walked over to the farmyard and leaned on the rough wood of the fence rail.

Star saw Will and trotted up to the fence. Her half-grown filly ran off on adventures of her own, chasing grasshoppers.

Henry patted the beautiful mare. "She's everything you said she was," he said. "And it looks like you'll have another foal, come spring."

"Pa's really worried about space and money," Will said, but he couldn't stop the grin that stretched across his face.

"Expanding a business is always risky," said

Henry. "But your Pa is careful. Well, he can count on your help. That's worth a lot." He clapped Will on the back and said his good-byes. Will watched Henry ride away, thinking of what he'd said.

Pa came up beside him, put one foot on the bottom fence rail and leaned his good arm on the top rail. The horses in the pasture all looked up, waiting to see if a pan of oats would be offered.

"Pretty sight, isn't it?" asked Pa. Will climbed up and sat on the top rail.

"Sure is." After a moment, he continued, "I've been thinking, Pa. I'm sure Mr. Davis would board Buck at the livery this winter in exchange for my working there after school. It shouldn't interfere with my chores here."

"That would work for a while," Pa said. "I've been doing some thinking myself."

Will looked down at him, curious. He wasn't sure what to expect of Pa anymore.

"When Mae and Molly foal in the spring, we'll be needing stall space. No way around it." He reached down and picked a long grass stalk and chewed on it. "When harvest is over, maybe we should start felling trees and take them to Geldner's Sawmill. Get enough lumber to make a good-sized stable. That'll leave the barn for the cattle."

"Yes!" said Will, almost losing his balance on the top rail. "We can get a rock foundation up this fall. Cut the trees right away, maybe those white oaks south of the wheat field. Good old Pete can haul logs like anything!"

Pa pushed away from the fence, smiling at Will's enthusiasm.

"It shouldn't cost too much," Pa said. "What worries me is paying Elmer Jones for stud fee for the Belgians next year." He walked back to the house.

Will thought about money and about Mr. Jones.

GETTING IT RIGHT
March 30, 1877

Moonlight glinted off icy puddles as Will crossed the yard, headed for the new stable. There had been a spring freeze overnight, and his breath condensed in the cold early morning air. The new double doors of the stable opened quietly. No more squeaky hinges. The horses, aware of him, stirred in their stalls. Star nickered a welcome.

Will lit the lantern and set it on its shelf. He stepped into the box stall, and the little filly shook her head as though to wake herself. Will slipped a little halter on her, led her out of the stall, and tied her to a post. She stood quietly as Will brushed her. Star poked her head over the half-door, watching.

"Have to have her looking her best, Star. We'll be saying good-bye to our little filly today." Will kept his voice low. He brushed bits of straw off the filly's sides and flanks, then turned and petted Star. He touched the white star on her forehead. "I knew raising horses would mean selling them. But I didn't think it would happen this soon or be this hard."

He walked to the next stall, where Buck had poked his head out the door to watch. Will saddled him and led him and the filly outside, extinguishing the lantern. The house was still dark when he rode past. He rode Buck down the drive at a brisk trot, leading the filly. She pranced and danced alongside. An early robin sang from the apple tree.

Riding the stallion always made Will feel good. He settled into Buck's rhythm and began to enjoy the sunrise, the sparkly glitter on frosty branches. They cantered the miles away, and the sun had turned the frosty earth to mud by the time Will arrived at Jones's farm.

White board fences enclosed pastures where large Belgian horses sunned themselves. A few Belgian mares nursed early spring foals. Will rode into the stable yard, and Mr. Jones came out to greet him. Will dismounted and shook his hand.

"Good morning, Will," called Mr. Jones. "What brings you here? Are your Belgian mares all right?

I recollect they're due to foal in April." He focused his attention on the filly. "Nice yearling you have there. Is she out of the mare you got from me?"

"The Belgians are doing just fine. We're right pleased with them," Will said. "This is Star's young'un. Bright as a new penny." He watched as Farmer Jones walked around the filly, eyes taking in every detail. Will hoped he'd think the filly was worth as much as stud service for Mae and Molly.

"We're thinking ahead to next year's foals, and stud service," Will began. "I had a trade in mind."

Farmer Jones ran a hand down the filly's legs, gently lifting each foot to inspect the hooves. He firmly raised her head and looked in her mouth. She stood obediently, on her best behavior. Will's training was paying off.

Mr. Jones motioned Will to walk her. Will led her around the stable yard, at different paces, reversing directions. The filly knew she was the center of attention, holding her head high, picking her feet up. Will knew Mr. Jones recognized her quality. But would he want a different breed on his stock farm? He had let Star go.

"I've been working her with a long line," said Will. "She's got a nice even trot. I had planned on putting light harness reins on her this summer. Just for training."

Jones nodded. "Wait here a minute," he said, and went into the stable. He came out leading a Belgian colt, half again as large as Will's filly. "I haven't done much with him except train him to lead," said Mr. Jones. "Too much stock here to spend as much time as I'd like on training."

Will stood stock-still, gazing at the handsome colt. It couldn't be any older than his filly.

"I'll make a proposition," said Farmer Jones. "The missus wants a buggy horse so she can go places by herself." He chuckled. "Doesn't want to use a big Belgian and a buckboard. How about an even trade, your filly for my stud colt here?"

Will felt stunned, then repressed a grin. An even trade? A stud colt for the little filly? That was better than he'd hoped for. He glanced at her again and saw just how lovely she was. Will handed her rope to Mr. Jones, then circled the Belgian colt to give it the same inspection he had just observed.

"Bred from your own stock?" he asked.

Pointing to a nearby corral, Mr. Jones said, "Out of yonder parents. Different line than your mares. He'll make a good breeding stallion for your Belgian herd. As for stud service this year," he continued, "if you could come over here to train your filly to drive, we'll call that an even trade."

Will didn't need to think long and hard. This was a solid trade. They shook hands to seal the bargain.

"What's her name?" asked Mr. Jones, patting the filly's neck. "The missus will want to know."

Will blinked a couple of times. "Um...," he said, then blurted out the first thing that came to mind, "Fancy. Her name's Fancy."

Mr. Jones chuckled. "Apt," he said. "The missus will like it." Fancy gave a dainty little snort and tossed her head. Will and Mr. Jones both laughed.

Will rode home leading the Belgian colt, who was every bit as playful as the filly had been, splashing exuberantly into puddles. He'd need a little work. A little settling down.

It was noon when Will arrived home. The snow had thawed and the air smelled of wet earth and wildflowers. He rode to the front porch and dismounted from Buck, keeping hold of the colt's lead rope. Ma and Pa came out on the porch, Ma still carrying a cast-iron skillet.

The colt stood bright-eyed and curious, surveying the barnyard. Pa stood on the top step looking him over, not saying anything.

Will held the lead rope firmly in his hand, looking up at Pa. "I made a trade with Mr. Jones, Pa. Star's filly for this colt. Even up." He sounded confident, sure it was a good trade. "I also traded services. I'll go to the Jones's farm and train the filly to drive in return for stud service for Mae and Molly."

Ma set the skillet on the top step and went down to fuss over the new colt. Pa came down the steps and walked slowly around the young stallion. He looked in its mouth and checked its hooves.

Will told Pa the colt's parentage. Pa nodded, standing back again. Will waited for Pa to speak.

"You made a fine trade, son. It shows good horse sense," Pa finally said, smiling at Will.

They all walked down to the pasture and Will turned Buck and the colt loose. The colt galloped around, tossing and shaking his head, then trotted up to the other horses to introduce himself.

Watching him from the gate, Ma said, "We'll have to think of a proper name for the youngster. Something fitting."

The colt trotted around the pasture and stopped abruptly for a drink in the creek. A frog jumped out from under his nose and the colt jumped back, startled. To cover his embarrassment, the colt chased around the pasture, bucking playfully.

"How about 'Rocky'?" said Will. "For rock-solid

horseflesh. Strong and dependable."

"Rocky," repeated Pa. "Rocky it is. Fits him, I think." Rocky was stomping on frogs by the creek.

Will, looking out over the pasture, felt very good. He watched Buck and Star nibbling fresh green shoots of grass. Star would foal soon. Will could hardly wait. Before long, he'd be naming another little foal.

He'd better give it some serious thought. Take his time. Get it right.

AUTHOR'S NOTE

In the summer of 1876, Minnesota celebrated the centennial anniversary of Independence Day. The Dakota Conflict was over, the Minnesota Volunteers had returned from the Civil War, and the state was looking forward to peace and prosperity.

Then, on September 7, the James-Younger outlaw gang rode into Northfield to rob the First National Bank. The brave citizens of Northfield foiled the robbery and the gang fled empty-handed. Two of its members, Clell Miller and Bill Stiles, were left dead in the street. The bank's acting cashier, Joseph Heywood, was killed when he refused to open the safe, and an innocent bystander, Nicolaus Gustafson, was also killed.

Many posses were formed to pursue the outlaws. At first they were unsuccessful, and it was thought the outlaws had all escaped. Then on September 13, the men were spotted near Mankato, Minnesota. The outlaw gang split up, and Frank and Jesse James were trailed all the way to the South Dakota border, where they escaped their pursuers.

No one really knows how Frank and Jesse eluded capture. The story about faking the jump over Devil's Gulch was told to me by a gentleman who lived his whole life in that area. As a child, he had heard the story from an older resident. A visit to the historical museum in Garretson, South Dakota, and the Palisades State Park made that story seem very real to me. Will's capture there, however, is all from my imagination.

Oscar Sorbel, a youngster who had been left to watch the Wawtowan River Bridge, spotted the three Younger brothers and Charlie Pitts on September 21. Oscar rode his father's workhorse into Madelia to alert authorities, and a local posse was formed, led by Sheriff Glispin. (Sheriff Barton's posse was not involved in that shoot-out.) The posse finally pinned down the outlaws in the bottomlands of the Wawtowan River. After a gun battle in which Charlie Pitts was killed, the badly wounded Younger brothers surrendered.

The Younger brothers pleaded guilty to the robbery and were sentenced to life in Stillwater Prison. Bob Younger died in prison. Jim and Cole were later paroled. The Youngers never divulged who killed Joseph Heywood. Cole did indeed write, "Be true to your friends till the heavens fall." Historians believe Frank James fired that fatal shot, though the presence of Frank and Jesse James and their participation in the Northfield bank robbery has never been proven. However, Jesse's grandson James A. Ross writes in his book *I, Jesse James*, that the James brothers were in Northfield and that Frank killed Joseph Heywood.

The characters of the outlaw gang are actual historical figures. Joseph Heywood, Nicolaus Gustafson, Alonzo Bunker, Henry Wheeler, Anselm Manning, and Sheriffs Barton and Glispin were also real people, as were a number of minor characters mentioned as Northfield citizens.

Will Sasse is based on an ancestor of mine who actually had his horse stolen after the Northfield robbery, but that's about all there is to that family history. Will and his parents' personalities, words, and actions are fictional. Will's relationship with the outlaws is also fiction. My nephew, however, still lives on the family farm where the outlaws first camped out.

The account of the bank raid, the dates of the robbery, and the posse activities are accurate. Cole's note and a revolver used in the robbery are on display in the Northfield Historical Museum, housed in the restored First National Bank. Every September, Northfield hosts a reenactment of the bank raid as part of its "Defeat of Jesse James Days."

CITATIONS

The quote from the *Rice County Journal* on page 148 is taken from a special edition of the *Northfield News* called "Defeat of the Jesse James Gang." The edition, edited by Maggie Lee, is made up of reprinted news reports, interviews, and other articles from many Minnesota newspapers.

BIBLIOGRAPHY

Books:

Breihan, Carl W. *The Complete and Authentic Life of Jesse James.* New York: Frederick Fell, 1953.

Breihan, Carl W. *The Escapades of Frank and Jesse James.* New York: Frederick Fell, 1974.

Lee, Maggie. *Defeat of the Jesse James Gang.* Northfield, MN: Northfield News, 1981.

Ernst, John. *Jesse James.* Englewood Cliffs, NJ: Prentice Hall, 1976.

Green, Carl R., and Sanford, William R. *Jesse James.* Hillside, NJ: Enslow Publishers, 1992.

Huntington, George. *Robber and Hero.* Northfield, MN: The Northfield Historical Society Press, 1994.

The Northfield Magazine, Vol. 6, No. 2, 1992.

Ross, James R. *I, Jesse James*. Thousand Oaks, CA: Dragon Publication Corporation, 1989.

Ross, Stewart. *Bandits and Outlaws*. Brookfield, CT: The Millbrook Press, 1995.

Documentaries:

"The Life of Jesse James and His Gang." *Biography: The Legends of the West*. Arts and Entertainment network, 1995.

There are also many commercial dramas, such as *The Long Riders, The Last Days of Frank and Jesse James, The Great Northfield, Minnesota Bank Raid*, and *Frank and Jesse*. None are historically accurate, but they are interesting for their flavor of the times.

A NOTE OF THANKS

I would like to thank my editor, Katy Holmgren, for her professional expertise and encouragement, Teri Martini for her help in crafting this novel, and Allison Cunningham for her expert advice in its first edit.

Thanks also to Susan Garwood-Delong, Executive Director of the Northfield Historical Society, for reading the manuscript for historical accuracy, and to Ken Berg for historical facts about 1870s Mankato; to the Arts Center of St. Peter, MN, and the McKnight Foundation (through Prairie Lakes Regional Arts Council) for financial support; and to my family for their encouragement. Thank you for oral histories from my mother, Olga Neubert, from Fred and Pat McKissack, from Bill Morris, Don Quiram, and from Dr. Dean Tieszen. Thanks to Dr. Rod Neubert, Dr. Rodney Revsbech, and my husband Duane for technical assistance on guns and horses. And of course, my fond appreciation to the Night Writers of St. Peter.

And most expecially, heartfelt thanks to Mary Casanova, Mentor Extraordinaire.

ABOUT THE AUTHOR

Jan Schultz lives with her husband on a farm homesteaded by the Schultz family in 1869, along the bluffs of the Minnesota River Valley. She is a fifth-generation Minnesotan and treasures the stories that have been handed down in her family.

Horse Sense is based on the story of an ancestor whose horse was stolen by the James-Younger gang after the Northfield bank raid.